Two Winters and 365 days

Two Winters and 365 days

Anuradha Prasad

PARTRIDGE
A Penguin Random House Company

To order additional copies of this book, contact
Partridge India
000 800 10062 62
www.partridgepublishing.com/india
orders.india@partridgepublishing.com

. . . Sometimes . . . angels live with us as family . . .

Thank you . . . Prasad and Riddhi . . .

Foreword

To all the women and men in the world who want to become someone . . .

Book I

WINTER

"We are calling from Route number 5. Is Rahul your husband?"

"Yes!"

"This is Los Angeles police . . . Who is this?"

"I am Ananya. Ananya. Please tell me? I am his, his . . . his wife. Ananya, his wife. Rahul's wife Ananya."

Ananya craned her ears to listen. She could not. Her words got swept by the blaring sirens.

"I am afraid ma'am . . . I am afraid," the male voice said. The bloody blaring sirens. They won't stop!

"Tell me please. I am Ananya. Tell me, speak to me please! Now!"

The sound of sirens was everywhere! The sound of her sobs mingled with the sirens. Sounds now became a part of her breath. She could feel all of it together inside her! She wanted to see, wanted to know. People were all around, swarmed around him, making a fuss. She saw him right there in the middle of the road, not moving, inert, lifeless! Could she? Could she? . . . Was he? Was he breathing? No!? Could she, could she breathe for Rahul? Her Rahul?

She bent down to touch him. He wouldn't move. "Rahul! Rahul!" He wouldn't breathe. "Rahul! Rahul!" He wouldn't turn. "Rahul! Rahul! Why don't you talk to me? Wake up, get up Rahul?!" The sirens blared louder. Rahul, sirens, police . . . blood . . . BLOOD!

Ananya sat up . . . drenched in cold sweat.

She looked around. The escaping morning breeze from the enclosed netted windows swung the white lace curtains gently. The soft cushions and bed covers of the same colour adorning the bed held her and her baby snugly in its comfort. The house looked peaceful in the morning light. The air conditioner produced a buzzing metallic sound. Ananya fell back on the cushions, strangely comforted by its sound.

Alia shifted sideways in her sleep. Her cherubic face was a carbon copy of Rahul. She looked so innocent and angelic in her soft cotton light blue tiny nightgown, oblivious to the world, reminding Ananya of her passionate love for Rahul. She stared at the ceiling. Her mind was not at rest, though her life had come to a standstill.

"You need to move on, dear," her American friend JJ had said when she had called from Los Angeles early that month to check on Ananya.

"Rahul was the centre of everything that I did, and he was a part of my . . . part of my very body . . . everything reminds me of him," Ananya had wailed over the phone.

"For the baby, Ananya! Give a chance to life for the baby's sake! TRY, TRY . . ." JJ had implored. "You can do it if you try!"

Ananya could feel that convulsing pain deep down in the pit of her stomach again, accompanied with a low feeling so akin to her nowadays with a sense of hopelessness. She stared at the ceiling, memories flooding back.

"We are calling from Route number 5, California Police. Can I speak to someone close to a gentleman called Rahul?"

Ananya's heart sank . . .

"I am, I am Rahul's wife, Ananya. I am Ananya. You can speak to me. Is Rahul in trouble?"

"I am afraid there is bad news. Your husband met with an accident!"

"Rahul met with an accident!? How? How? How did it happen? I mean how did he? Oh my God! How?" Ananya slipped to the floor, almost fainting. "I want to talk to him now!"

"I am afraid, ma'am." There was a long pause.

"Hello? Hello? Officer? Hello!?"

"He is no more!"

Ananya took a deep breath.

She looked at the bedside table. Out of the many frames, Rahul smiled at her. She was laughing with him in one, on her wedding day. She was happy in all the pictures with him. She gingerly placed a finger on the handsome face, tears rolling down.

"Why did you leave me? Why did you have to leave me? Rahul?! I cannot live! Live without you! I just cannot." Her chest heaved in heavy sobs. Convulsions rocked her as she thought, 'Why? Why, Rahul?' Now the convulsion rose to her gullet, choking her. She pushed her face into the pillows. Her body rocked.

"Why did you leave me alone?" This she must have asked hopelessly millions of times. Her baby moved in her sleep again.

Ananya slid out of the bed covers, hugging the wedding picture to her chest. The marble felt warm under her feet. She moved to the other bedroom with tears rolling down her cheeks. She looked at Rahul. He just smiled back. The olive green and yellow baby nursery rocked around her till she could not stand it any more. She ran to the bathroom and threw up in the pot.

After what seemed like an eternity, Ananya splashed cold water from the tap and stood holding the side of the sink. The plush baby crib with soft satin-cotton American blankets in yellow, olive green, and blue stared back at her.

She walked out of the bathroom and sat on the edge of the bed. She pulled the picture to her chest again.

Rahul was super crazy about kids.

"I want a whole football team, no less," he had said after kissing her passionately at the Mumbai airport before proposing to her.

"We are not supposed to kiss in public places, especially in the airport car parking," she had joked, laughing.

He had pulled her close, and they had gone on a kissing spree again. They were there to pick up one of his friends from abroad.

"I cannot promise you anything, Rahul. I am supposed to be at a party," she had laughed, pulling away. "If my parents find out about us, you will have to plan marriage with someone else."

"I will never get married to anyone except you," he had proclaimed passionately.

She looked at the picture through her moist eyes. It looked a little blurred; she gingerly placed her lips and pecked Rahul on the cheek as if he were a real person. "Rest!" she said, weeping . "Rest!"

"We will go abroad for some years after marriage. As I am an architect, I can make a lot of money, and we will come back!"

"Why back?"

"I love Mumbai."

"Me too," she had rejoined happily.

"I will come to your place to ask for your hand."

"Great! Can we get out of the car park?"

"No! Not so soon." His head had come down for another passionate kiss that lasted for quite some time.

She moved a finger on his handsome picture now.

This modest two-bedroom apartment in Thakur Village, a western suburb in Mumbai, was an investment Rahul had made before they shifted base to Los Angeles.

Ananya carefully adjusted the sleeping bags on the protective bedding on the small baby cot that she had got from abroad.

'Now I have no use of them in this warm Mumbai weather.' she thought. 'Now everything is over, no going back, no more of an American dream. It's over with Rahul.'

She had sold off their state home in the United States to pay the debts Rahul had taken to buy it, and now she was back forever.

"That is what you would have wanted, isn't it?" she asked Rahul's picture. "You will never talk to me, will you? You only smile back!"

She held the frame close to her chest and heaved into a sobbing oblivion one more time.

Her wailing baby woke her at 9.30.

"Oh! The diaper is wet!" Ananya carried Alia and went back into the baby's room and fished for some in the cupboard.

'The diapers that I got from the United States are getting over,' she thought groggily.

Alia was unleashing a pandemonium by now. She hated to be in wet diapers. Ananya made Alia lie down on the baby bed and changed her into a fresh one, crooning a lullaby groggily.

Once in the fresh diaper, Alia was gurgling ecstatically.

Ananya picked up Alia in a stupor and walked to the front door, singing her soft little American baby song. Six-month-old Alia sang along.

"Hush-a-bye, hush-a-bye, you sweet little baby . . . don't you cry, don't you cry, you little baby."

"Gurgle . . . gurgle . . . mumuumm," sang Alia.

"Daddy has gone to his stockbroker's office keeping, the wolf from the door . . . door door."

"Mmmmuuummgggargglee."

"Nursie will raise the window shade high, so you can see the cars whizzing by."

"Gaaarrgglee ummm."

"Home in a hurry, each daddy must fly to a baby like you . . . a baby like you."

"GAAAARRRRGGLLEEEE."

Ananya collected the milk packets from the door.

Her neighbours, Mrs Mishra and Mrs Verma, were chatting away animatedly. Both were middle-aged housewives. Ananya had not interacted much with them in the past three months since she had shifted to the neighbourhood. They were generally very sweet and offered help whenever she asked them. Mrs Verma even gave Ananya her general physician's number for emergencies. If they saw that Ananya was little disturbed and remained alone, they never asked personal questions.

They smiled at Ananya now and made a sweet face at Alia.

"Good morning!" Ananya greeted them softly from the door.

"Good morning!" they responded.

Ananya came to the kitchen with the milk packets. She had a checklist on the kitchen reminder board that she followed religiously every day.

The items on the list read as:

> Call up the milkman for more milk.
> Clean the cupboards.
> Get some supplies for the kitchen.
> Check with the neighbours for a good house help.
> (The house help she had now was irregular). She put the milk for heating. At the end of the list was
> Call up Amanda again!

Amanda Miller was Ananya's best friend from college. Ananya had kept in touch with her through mails and calls whenever she was in Mumbai or abroad. Failing finances worried Ananya. She repeated to herself, 'Today I must call up Amanda without fail!'

The place went dark. The kaleidoscopic lights flashed colourful loud patterns on the ramp. The smoke machines whizzed away. In the shadows stood a model invisible to the audience. The whole place went silent. A moment later, the music started. The models walked slowly from the shadows with their male counterparts. The ramp dazzled. The Fall/Winter Collection Show 2012 had started. High-society men and women were hungry for new fashion. Film stars ogled for fresh designs, producers and directors sat there to spot fresh faces, and camera men almost fell on each other for a better angle. The place was rampant with make-up artists, fashion photographers, designers, live channels covering up the event, and last but not the least THE PRESS.

Amanda was in the crowd too. In a red short skirt—'formal suit'—that accentuated her flamboyant personality. She was in her late twenties and had large inquisitive black eyes, thick curly hair of the same colour, and a dusky complexion. She was short, plump, and bossy. She was a very senior journalist from *Our Times* an outstanding national newspaper, and had been recently promoted to an editorial position. With all this, to boot, she had something rare that most media people lacked—A GOLDEN HEART!

Today, she had got a special invite to attend the Fall/Winter collection of one of the famous designers in town—Gurmeet Salhotra. She was accompanied by her colleague Prateek. There was a short break after the initial round.

Amanda was sitting bang in front of the ramp. It was a regular T-ramp that is generally erected for fashion shows. First seats were always reserved for the press, and she was promptly there on time.

"Prateek, we are able to watch the models from here so well," she declared, all the while playing with her puffy ponytail at the top of her head.

"Ya, ma'am, good place," Prateek agreed. He could not take his eyes off her colourful, bold nail art.

"Oberoi Mall," she informed him. "Great art, no?" she asked, winking.

Prateek was this flirtatious young junior, a fresh graduate in his early twenties, full of life and spunk; he mostly flattered his seniors to be in their good books.

"I am so impressed that I cannot take my eyes off them—your nails."

The media was full of younger guys falling for older women.

Amanda playfully said, "Prateek, no taking chances with me, eh? Eh? No younger guy business for me."

"No, ma'am. I was only admiring you. Am I not allowed?" he protested in mock pain.

"Oh God! You are," she rejoined in mock seduction. The music started again for the next round, and the lights dimmed.

Amanda saw the red light on her dicta blinking. "I am not going to use my Dictaphone here. Waste of battery," she said and put it out. "We need it to take the interviews of the models backstage. Prateek, you switch off yours."

He did.

Both of them concentrated now on the show with their pencils and pads.

The models started walking again now in the latest Indian design wear, dominated with Anarkali-patterned Indian *chudidars* of kaleidoscopic colours. They had outlandish hairstyles and very big nails with beautiful nail art.

"Look, Prateek, the nails, they have amazing art on them!" Amanda said in whispers.

Prateek, who was equally enjoying his day out with Amanda and the fashion models, bent forward dramatically to whisper that hers were the best!

Amanda playfully pushed his face away.

For some time they took notes of the attires on the show quietly.

Amanda recognised some of the models and was excited.

"She is Hetal, and she is Mahek. They are top models. Look, here comes Remo. God! He's lost so much weight from the last I saw him."

Prateek, of course, was nodding away at everything she said.

Most of the models in traditional outfits wore dazzling clothes in true Bollywood style, complete with golden coins and *ghungroo kamarbandhs*. Amanda made a note of the beautiful long *Anarkali kurtis* that blended in so well with the *chudidar* tights underneath. Prateek followed suit, smiling.

She nudged her young junior playfully with her elbow, asking him not to copy her style.

He moved his head to show he was not.

There was a short two-minute break again after the traditional Indian round.

"The words of a journalist need to be as flamboyant as the clothes on the show," she preached to her colleague.

He agreed, flattering her, and said that he was learning a lot in her company.

Amanda threw a look at him with a twinkle in her eye as the lights dimmed one more time for the next round.

Bright colours, evening gowns, flairs, chiffons, crepes, *zari,* embroidered borders, and modern cuts were prominent in a majority of the clothes. Beautiful hand-loom fabrics were turned into Western tunics of unimaginable contours and shapes. There were tapering long evening gowns, made out of multicoloured saris, in all combinations and styles with tons of layers.

"Most of the dresses are not practical," Prateek commented in between.

"True! But they are the fashion worn by high society," Amanda whispered.

At that point, Hetal entered wearing a long primrose chiffon evening gown teamed with a gold-and-silver bustier. This time she was with another male model, whom Amanda could not recognise. At least six models were displaying their garments one after the other, swinging to the reverberating music. It was Hetal's turn now; she walked to the front, one leg before the other, with a huge pout and a super huge attitude. She walked right to the centre of the spotlight and posed at an angle. At that moment, her bustier gave way!

Prateek let out a cry, and the whole place went into shock for a few minutes. The photographers started clicking non-stop. It was a couple of seconds before the model realised what had gone wrong. Some people smirked, letting out ghastly sighs, hiding their faces behind each other's backs.

Hetal pulled the bustier up her chest with a sweep; her face was emotionless and wooden, but the colour on it said it all! The expression, Amanda could tell, came from long training on the ramp. Hetal completed her act and went backstage. The audience was in shock for some time, and as she left, there were animated discussions on the act! The show went on as scheduled.

As Hetal went backstage, a storm of activity broke. She just dropped to the floor, weeping. The designers covered her, and fellow models sympathised with her.

#

Amanda reached her office late in the afternoon next day after the high-profile party at Hyatt and the fashion show the previous day. She was walking to her glass cabin when she overheard Ashlesha and Neha.

"They were found in his bathroom. The other day the lady was in his lap." Ashlesha and Neha were writers with *Our Times*.

Amanda retraced her steps backwards . . .

"Who was in whose lap?" Amanda asked them.

"I had been to a press house somewhere in town, and there was this affair going on between the junior staff and the chief editor. The woman is found everywhere with him. They are found kissing in the bathrooms. She was in his lap after office hours."

"You guys are lucky I am a woman," Amanda chuckled.

Ashlesha and Neha laughed. "True, otherwise to save our jobs, we would have ended up the same way," remarked Neha.

"The newspapers are agog with yesterday's wardrobe malfunction," observed Ashlesha. "Ma'am, you were at the venue with Prateek at the show?"

"It could be a publicity gimmick for all we know," added Sumit from an adjoining cubicle. He was their subeditor.

"Oh, you awake?" Amanda joked. "I don't think so. The poor girl was in tears after the show," she added.

There were at least twenty newspapers on the table reporting about the fashion week mishap. Some were callous, some kind, some indifferent.

"Poor thing," commented Amanda again.

"Don't say that, ma'am! The other day, at the Mumbai press party, there was this starlet without her undergarments," added Sumit. "Publicity gimmick! 100 per cent!" He moved his head.

"Actually," rejoined Neha, "scary, no?"

"The press had a field day though, clicking away at the poor girl!" Amanda rejoined.

"The whole media was agog about the girl with no underpants," Sumit added again with a lot of interest.

The girls exchanged glances and made faces at Sumit's consistent statements at "no undergarments" story.

By now, Amit, their peon, was standing in a corner to catch Amanda's attention.

"That story could be a publicity gimmick, not this. I at least don't think so," Amanda observed and asked Amit, "Do you want something? Amit *bhaiya*?"

"*Haan*, madam, the same boy has come for the interview."

"Oh! OK, let him sit. I will go to my cabin." Amanda turned to others, "The same guy. You remember? I have called him today again. We so badly need reporters here."

"Yes! That boy, no?" Ashlesha asked.

"I took his interview the other day. He is good," added Sumit.

"Ask him to sit," Amanda repeated to hovering Amit.

Amanda went to her cabin. The same twenty newspapers stared back at her. It was a general practice that Amit followed day in and day out, dutifully placing every newspaper in town fanned out on her table, bringing the news about the world. She moved her head in disgust.

'Poor girl!' she said to herself. At the same time, her mobile rang! It was Ananya . . .

"Yes, darling, what's up?" Amanda asked absently with an eye still on the papers.

"I really wanted to connect with you today again. Hope I am not disturbing you?" Ananya's voice worried Amanda nowadays. 'She sounds so low,' she thought and added jovially, "You are, but I can spare five minutes for you. Hi, hi."

Immediately Ananya's voice went down. "Sorry, I will call you some other . . ."

"No, sweetie, please talk. I can always spare you at least five minutes every day," Amanda said in her high-handed fashion again.

At this point, Amit came to her cabin with a fresh cup of coffee and a complaint on his face. "Madam . . . interview?"

"Excuse me!" Amanda said in the phone.

Ananya heard Amanda speak to someone. "*Haan, Amit?*"

"Interview, madam," he said, dragging his voice.

"Ask the boy to sit for five minutes, *na*? I will call him after five." She signalled with her open palm to Amit, 'five'. Amanda signalled after him . . . with her palm again . . . "Five, five, you understand?" she repeated as he walked out with a complaining face.

"Sorry, dear!" said Amanda, coming back on the line.

Ananya asked hesitatingly, "How are you? It's been a month since we spoke so I . . . er . . ."

"I am fine. How is your little one, baby?" Amanda addressed people close to her as darlings and babies in her characteristic style. "Dear, you need not be so formal with me."

"She is good. My baby is good." The sheer lack of confidence in Ananya's voice shook Amanda.

"Yes, angel?" Amanda said aloud and thought about her friend. 'She has changed so much! Not the Ananya I knew! Nowadays always quiet and sad!' The last time she had visited Ananya (that was a month back), Amanda was taken aback by her dark circles and swollen eyes. She looked worried and was talking all the time, about some financial problems.

"I just called to say hi!" Ananya was saying.

"Hi, then," said Amanda, mocking her. "Talk darling! You are welcome."

"If it's not out of the way, umm . . . if you remember I had spoken to you about finding something for me."

"Something for you? Something for you? Ummm?Oh shit! I am sorry!" Amanda just slumped in her chair with a hand to her head. "Damn! I was so busy, it just slipped from my mind. Ananya darling, will you do me a favour? Can you send me your updated CV?"

"Yes, but there is nothing to update in it."

"Ummm . . . you have a graduation in English Literature, and you were the star editor of our college magazine, right? Remember? You don't, but I do. So write, my dear girl, that you got the Best Editor's inter-collegiate award, what else?" Amanda added brightly to bring up Ananya's spirit.

"That was so long, long ago. I am out of touch now." The sheer lack of confidence in Ananya's voice was draining Amanda.

"You are a major in English Literature, darling. I am just a Mass Media graduate. I am doing quite well. You will too." Amanda encouraged her.

"Yes, but I am not sure, Amanda, about myself. I am not confident. I am very nervous these days." Amanda started sipping coffee, as her heart bled for her best friend's condition. She remembered her till last year, as a bubbly and a cheerful housewife. 'How time changes people?' Amanda thought.

"I have not gone out of the house for five years, Amanda. I have only been a housewife all these years."

"Ummm! Let me think. What about teaching?"

"In fact, I had got a couple of teaching offers in schools nearby through the help of my neighbours. They are paying very less as I have no experience and no training." Ananya's confidence was at the lowest of the low.

Amanda remembered Ananya's mom and her dog collars, which she so often used to joke about in college. (Ananya's mom retired as a teacher from one of Mumbai's schools. She had to wear dog collars to correct papers by the end of her career because of cervical spondylosis. After her retirement, she had moved to London permanently to stay with her son after selling her properties in the town.)

"Besides, you will end up in a dog collar," Amanda was saying to lighten the situation.

"Oh yes! Actually teaching reminds me of Ma's dog collars." Ananya smiled for the first time in the day. "Now that Mom is retired, I don't want to show her how broke I am. She will be worried."

"True, dear," agreed Amanda. "Looking into your situation with a baby, I would recommend a part-time job."

"A part-time job? I need a decent salary to run my house." Ananya's voice trailed.

"I can only get you a media-related job, and that means long hours in the office. I will see what I can do." As she was talking, she could hear Alia's wail in the background. Amanda's stomach churned.

"A nine-to-five job I do not mind." Ananya persisted hopelessly. "An office job if you can get me? Anything." Ananya's voice sounded almost like a wail.

Amit again came to the door with his complaining face.

Amanda showed him her five fingers. He went away smirking.

"Yes, Ananya, media and journalism for you will be taxing," Amanda said, "but I will try my best to find an easy option with a good pay package, most ideally. Now I must hang up, dear. Some people are hanging outside my door."

"OK, dear."

"Take care, darling!"

Amanda signalled Amit to send in the candidate.

A short, plump, odd looking boy of twenty-two came in with his CV. He was a BMM graduate from one of the top colleges of Mumbai. He had cleared the preliminary two rounds with HR and the subeditor's panel. Amanda just wanted to check on him personally. After a few minutes with him, she felt that he had the much-needed hunger for the post and the soft skills required for the job. She also observed that the boy was sober and very calm (one of the added prerequisites).

She smiled to herself, thinking, 'But, he has such big ears, like Mickey Mouse.'

"Mickey Mouse sat in his chair inside his house in Mickey's Toontown Fair." Ananya was reading to Alia. Alia clapped, swinging from side to side. This was the favourite time of the day with her mommy.

"Gggrrrrggrrlleeee," she gurgled in response, moving her tiny toes on Tigressá, a soft American carpet laid out in the living room. The whole of the living room was strewn with soft toys, construction cubes of different shapes and colours, and storybooks of all imaginable sizes with cartoon characters peeking out of them. It was around eleven in the morning, and after Alia's bath and feed, she was in a mood for story reading.

Ananya, in her nightgown, squatted on the carpet along with Alia, reading out and acting and mimicking while she read. These were Ananya's golden moments with her baby. She read next:

"Then the evil Rattigan has an evil plan." Ananya's voice rose, so did Alia's gurgle.

"Oooooooo." Alia made a face and put out her lips in a pout as Ananya read with expression.

Alia pointed to some Mickey Mouse pictures.

Ananya explained, "Alia, look, look, baby, Mickey Mouse. Mickey Mouse has big ears, baby, big ears." Ananya pointed towards her own ears and Alia's.

Alia mimicked her, "BBBBBLLLLLee," and showed the picture in a mock expression of reading putting together her lips again.

Ananya just smacked the little forehead, and her baby clapped again with glee.

Alia was over six months and could sit on her own, clap, and gurgle. 'She is slowly getting used to the humid Mumbai weather too!' Ananya observed.

The reading continued with a lot of hand expressions and gestures. Little Alia copied her mom.

"To capture Mickey, Rattigan made a plan."

"Garrlllee." The doorbell rang.

"Then Mickey Mouse heard someone at the door," Ananya read out.

The doorbell rang again. Ananya went on.

"Then Mickey Mouse went outside and saw the evil Rattigan."

The doorbell rang again.

Ananya got up this time to go to the door, and little Alia in her pink frock, white diapers, and red bands, signalled excitedly towards the door, thinking it to be a part of the act.

Mrs Verma and Mrs Mishra were at the door. Mrs Mishra had a home-baked cake on a platter in her hands.

"We wanted to formally invite you to our neighbourhood."

"Oh! Please, please come in," said Ananya, surprised. "It was unnecessary."

"No, no! You see, Mrs Mishra and I were watching this American serial," Mrs Verma said. "Some housewives. Umm, I am unable to recall . . . ummm," she said, making herself comfortable on the cushiony sofa immediately.

Mrs Mishra came in and stood with the cake near the dining table. "*Desperate Housewives,*" she reminded Mrs Verma.

"Oh yes! Of course!" Ananya said.

"You know, we watch that serial together every Friday and Saturday," informed Mrs Mishra. "In one episode, a lady is invited to the neighbourhood with a home-baked cake, so we thought of this idea."

"You are from America, no? We thought you will like it," added Mrs Verma, very happy at her novel idea.

"It was unnecessary," Ananya rejoined again, softly.

Alia, by now, sensing Ananya's distraction, started to whimper, pointing to her storybook.

"Please sit down," requested Ananya to Mrs Mishra, who was still standing at the table.

"*Haan, haan,* first take the cake," said Mrs Mishra, putting it on the dining table.

At that point, Ananya mentioned to the ladies that she was, in fact, planning to visit them with a request for a good maid as Sanjana (the present maid) was very irregular. Both Mrs Verma and Mrs Mishra offered to help Ananya readily. Minutes later, with Alia in her arms, Ananya went into the kitchen to make some coffee for her guests.

After a while, Mrs Mishra followed Ananya into the kitchen and exclaimed,

"Why are you making coffee, dear?"

"Because we will have the chance to eat the cake together," Ananya rejoined in good humour. "That you so lovingly made!" They exchanged amicable smiles.

Mrs Mishra went out and landed herself next to Mrs Verma again, and they animatedly discussed the American lifestyle, weather, maidservants, and pests in the building. Both were middle-aged, typical Indian housewives. Mrs Mishra had two teenaged children, one boy and a girl in college, while Mrs Verma's children were abroad. Both wore the same kind of *salwar kurtees*, jeans, and T-shirts, even saris and went out shopping together and to watch movies; they were inseparable.

"Nice pots," observed Mrs Mishra, looking at Ananya's gallery. "Nice home, very neat! No cockroaches, it seems?"

"She is from America, no? She must be used to a lot of cleanliness," added Mrs Verma. "My daughter's home also very, very clean, so is my son's. No pollution, no, in America," added Mrs Verma.

"Aaaan . . . I see . . . true!" agreed Mrs Mishra.

Ananya's mobile started ringing, and Alia's whimpers increased.

"Here, give her to me," said Mrs Verma, coming into the kitchen, and Mrs Mishra followed her.

"I will make coffee. You please attend your mobile," Mrs Mishra offered.

It was Amanda.

"Hi, Amanda," Ananya wished. "Good morning!"

Amanda thought, 'Ananya sounds a little cheerful today.'

"Hey, how you been, girl?"

"Good, I think."

"Hey! I have something for you as requested."

"Something?" Ananya asked. "You mean, you mean, a job?"

"Yep! Exactly," Amanda agreed. "You cannot get luckier, girl."

Alia was screaming from the kitchen by now, pushing herself away from Mrs Verma's hands; her eyes on Ananya.

"I guess I need to be fast. Your baby is crying."

"No, no, don't bother, please tell me."

"You know, a friend of my friend is looking for someone to edit his magazine."

"Edit? That's like?" Ananya said uncertainly.

"Like, they want an editor for their magazine, simple! I recommended your name, simple!"

"What? My name?" Ananya said incredulously "How do I . . . ?" Her voice faltered.

"Sweetheart, they want a full-time editor. I recommended your name. The interview is day after." Amanda breathed out the entire information fast.

Ananya's heart missed a beat. She was not expecting something like this.

"Oh! Umm! What is this magazine? Amanda, you know very well that I don't have any editing experience."

By now Alia was howling loudly. Mrs Verma came with her into the sitting room and gave her to Ananya.

Amanda said, "Day after 'morrow, you need to be there at twelve." Alia was quiet now, looking at her mom with wet eyes and a snug expression on her face.

"But, Amanda, you know that I am not experienced and . . .".

Mrs Verma got a cup of piping hot coffee for Ananya from the kitchen and put it under her nose.

"Have it!" she whispered.

Ananya took it from her. "Thank you!"

"You said thank you to me? That's great, girl. Then you are going to the interview?" Amanda joked.

"No, it was for my neighbour who gave me coffee."

"Oh!" Amanda pretended frustration. "Great! You have to go anyways for the interview day after at twelve o'clock. I have spoken to them. They will be waiting for you, right?"

"But editing?!"

"No ifs and no buts," her friend said sternly.

"What is the magazine about? At least tell me something?"

"Darling! It is a lifestyle magazine based at Andheri, not far from your place. Though it's a full-time job, you will not be stressed much as it's a monthly publication. I thought of everything, then spoke to them."

"Umm! Oh! But how . . . will I?"

"Yep! You were the best editor of our college, remember, girl?"

"That was just a college magazine, and this is?"

"This is lifestyle. I thought it was just right for you at this point. There is no harm in giving it a try, honey," Amanda forced her.

"Ummm," Ananya said doubtfully. "But do they know anything about me?"

"I prepared a rough CV of yours and mailed them," Amanda said.

"You did that? Who does that? Oh God!" Ananya wailed, and Alia reciprocated. "Garrrllleee!" She was cranky and unhappy still about the disturbance in her enjoyable story-telling.

"I do that! Amanda does that!" Amanda rejoined in the same tone as Ananya.

"Oh God! Amanda, I am not sure if I can do this. I mean, editing—it is asking for too much!"

"First thank me?" Amanda said in mock offence.

"Thank you!" Ananya said.

"Garrlee tatattaaata," Alia said, clapping.

"Ta-ta, ta-ta," Amanda laughed. "Alia is saying ta-ta to me. Chao for now! I will hang up." She added, "Dear, your sentences are always full of buts and cant's these days. First, go to the interview, work, then see, who knows? You might like it. Give it a go, girl. Day after, remember." Amanda stressed, with no space for further protests from her friend.

"I? Where do I?"

"Leave everything to me," Amanda said, dominating the talk. "Don't worry! Life does not present you with opportunities every day. Now I need to go to a meeting. Bye! Love you!"

"I love you!" Amanda's boyfriend said and kissed her passionately again.

"Don't! Ummm!" She pushed him away, complaining, "We have not even brushed."

Siddharth was Amanda's live-in boyfriend. It was early Monday morning and both needed to rush to work.

"Please come here." Siddharth pulled her by her arm again as she was sitting on the edge of the bed, struggling with her bra hook.

"Come here, I will put it for you." Siddharth went over and pulled her to him, feeling her all over again.

"Liar!" She hit at him.

"You look more beautiful in the mornings with all the messed-up hair and that sleepy expression. I just cannot resist."

"After making out all night and every hour messing up again and again?" she laughed softly.

"Yes," he rejoined, ecstatic at the thought of the golden lovemaking hours.

"We need to go to work," Amanda protested.

"There is still time, baby," he complained, pulling her to him and holding her in a vice-like grip.

"Oh, don't!" she said, putting up her nose at him as he came closer.

He pulled a mouth freshener from under his pillow and sprayed himself, crushing her lips underneath his once more.

"You animal!" she spat out. They romped for some time, indulging in heavy petting. Amanda nuzzled up close to Siddharth after a while and said, "I need to check on the children. It's been a while."

Her children were a couple of toddlers she had adopted from a Mumbai orphanage. One was only a year old and the other was two and a half years old and attended a play-school nearby. The adoption was an outcome of Amanda's many interviews for her paper three years back about child abuse in orphanages. She was extremely moved by the plight of poor orphans in the city and had decided on adoption. Her mom and dad living nearby were not proud of Amanda at first, but as time passed, they had no option but to accept Siddharth and the kids as a part of their daughter's life. Now, her family was complete with a golden Labrador and a live-in maid to take care of everybody.

"Hush, hush! There is still a lot of time for Sahil's school," Siddharth said, pulling her further into the bed covers. (Sahil was their adopted son, and his name started with S like Siddharth; Anupa was their daughter, and her name started with A like Amanda.)

The previous night, Siddharth had come home very late in the wee hours, and since then, they were in the room, locked up!

Siddharth and Amanda's love story was like a Bollywood romance. Amanda had hit on him full after they met at a media promo party that he had attended with a friend from Bollywood. He was a banker, and Amanda was a fiery journalist with unearthly working hours. When they fell in love, they decided to live together. Since Siddharth did not have a house of his own, he moved in with Amanda, into her huge four-bedroom terrace flat in Film City, Goregaon—East. Both had erratic working hours playing spoilsport with their love lives, but it was four years now, and they were still going strong. Amanda was non-committal about marrying, while Siddharth was OK with whatever arrangement she thought was right for them. His parents lived in Delhi, and they had no option but to accept Siddharth's life as part of modern living. On his part, he was happy that he was with the woman he loved.

Amanda twisted out of the blankets.

"Oh shit, it is 7.46, and I need to go to Thakur Village pick up Ananya and her baby. I had promised to drive her to Oshiwara today and back. She has no one here, except me to help her."

Siddharth remembered Amanda mentioning something about picking up Ananya for an interview. "What time is the interview?" he asked.

"Twelve."

"Lotta time," he said, lighting a cigarette with one arm still around Amanda.

Amanda took a long drawl at the cigarette, filling her lungs with the smoke, and disentangled herself and started dressing up again.

"Here! Siddharth put the hook for her this time."

"What time do you plan to go to work?"

"Umm, let me see," he said. "I am little groggy after yesterday's flight. I might sleep for some more time."

"I need to check with Ranjeeta about the food today. We have two little ones instead of one at home. Alia, Ananya's baby, will be staying the day with us," added Amanda.

Siddharth's face softened.

"You need to take her itinerary first. She happens to be a special American baby."

"True! Now I need to brush, shower and dress, then oversee the breakfast and check on the babies. Sahil's teacher was talking about making him learn some Sanskrit verse that she had written in his diary for homework."

"Sanskrit verse?"

"Yes. They are incorporating it as a part of induction to Indian culture for the school children nowadays. I suppose."

"Really?"

"Yep." Amanda added, "After picking Ananya and her baby, I need to come home, drop Alia with Ranjeeta (their servant), then take Ananya to her interview. All that's later. First I need to brush, shower, dress, and look at the little one. Anupa slept yesterday night very late because of the cough. I gave her some cough syrup, which must have made her sleep longer."

Siddharth said, "I will look after the kids. You get ready. I will oversee the breakfast till you get dressed." By now, Amanda had worn her loose tee and some pyjamas from the night before. She found the used condoms on the floor.

Siddharth saw them too. "I will take care of everything. First get ready, darling."

She mimicked him with her nose up in the air. "I will look after everything, darling! First, dress up, darling. You are naked, darling!" she laughed lightly.

With the blankets around his midriff, Siddharth just took another long drawl as he watched Amanda dress with lusty lazy eyes, without bothering about 'dressing up.' She went out of the room, closing the door behind her softly.

Ananya opened the door only a slit for Amanda to come in.

Ananya had just thrown a bathrobe on to open the door for her friend. She was dripping wet!

"Dear, I was in the shower. Please make yourself comfortable," said she in whispers with only an eye open, as the dripping shampoo was smarting her eyes.

"Where is Alia?" Amanda asked with enthusiasm immediately after she landed herself in.

Ananya put a finger to her mouth, signalling her friend to be quiet.

Amanda stiffened. "What the f#%*#&*?"

"Hush, hush, Alia is sleeping, dear. Not well, I have given her the cough syrup," Ananya informed her in whispers.

Amanda nodded, signalling with her hands excitedly in return and whispering that Ananya had lost weight. She also informed her about her own baby's ill health.

"Oh! It must be the changing weather," Ananya said, worried, and asked, "Did I lose weight really?" Though she knew that loneliness and lack of sleep were the culprits!

"Yes!" rejoined Amanda, winking.

Ananya was making a pool where she stood. She excused herself. "I will be back in a jiffy! Be my guest and please pour some juice for yourself from the fridge!" She ran back into the bathroom.

"Yep! Don't worry, take your time, angel. In the meanwhile, I will see what you have done to the house!" Amanda said in a hoarse whisper.

Amanda loved beautiful homes. She had an amazing sense of decor herself.

She looked around. The long French glass windows opened out to a narrow long terrace, spotted with multicoloured pots of colourful leafy indoor plants. She recognised begonia, a perennial flowering plant that she had at her own home in Goregaon. The pots of begonia were full of red-pink flowers, giving the space a cheerful look. The balcony was neat and tidy, and it was also accessible from one of the bedrooms. Amanda stood there, filling her lungs with fresh air that had a lingering tinge of the morning chill.

"Beautiful! There is so much of greenery out here," she exclaimed to herself. "What a view!" From the sixteenth floor of Ananya's home, the whole of Thakur Village was visible.

She was still groggy from previous day's romping sleepless night with Siddharth. She smiled to herself at the very thought of him. She checked the time in her mobile. It was 9.30. 'I should be able to reach Ananya on time if we start here by ten,' she calculated.

She walked back into the hall, kicking her sandals out. The marble felt warm.

She stood for some seconds, admiring the long double-net curtains of white and cream, white-and-black chequered Tigressá soft American carpet, and the cream walls with rich and expensive imported artefacts. A long showcase of light wood with sunglass adorned the wall opposite to the windows; it was replete with imported photo frames of family pictures and had a huge television over it. The decor of the living room was warm, simple, yet rich and inviting.

'I will pour myself a drink,' she decided and sauntered into the kitchen. She took a wine goblet from an open shelf and poured herself a mango juice from a Tetra Pack.

The walls of the kitchen were white. The tiles were of olive green, embossed with dark green wine creepers and maroon grapes. The cabinets of olive green colour had tiny focus lights peeking from the corners. A small American three-legged light wooden table with tiny chairs on either side was in a corner. A wooden focus light came down on it.

'A table for two?' Amanda pondered. 'How romantic!'

She pulled a chair and sat down, drinking the juice from the wine goblet. She gingerly ran a palm, feeling the soft fabric of the red-and-white chequered table cloth with white crochet work on the edges. Innumerable dining sets and cutlery peeked at Amanda from the cabinets above. The warm morning breeze with the smells of winter bloom wafted from the open windows. The sunlight made patterns on the floor, reflecting the designs from the focus light above.

The house had a slightly damp smell to it. Amanda decided that the smell complimented the antique furniture in the house.

'I need some ice in it!' She opened the fridge to fill her drink with ice cubes.

'Now my drink is on the rocks!' She lifted the glass in an imaginary toast. 'To Ananya and her bright future!'

Walking back into the hallway, she took a glance at the pink fox and beaver carved from Mexican wood. 'This is a Nahnal snail from Mexico . . . I have read about it somewhere,' she told herself. Cushiony off-white classic three-piece sofa set and a four-seater simple dining table completed the decor. The seating area looked large because of the minimal furniture.

A miniature landscape was in the corner of the dining space with the provision for a fountain. Amanda was observing it when she jumped at Ananya's voice.

"This was a gift from Rahul on my last birthday." Ananya had come out of the bath in a bathrobe and a towel wrapped around her head. "He knew how crazy I was for artefacts."

"Wow, it is gorgeous," Amanda responded aloud, forgetting to whisper.

Ananya said softly in response, "It's 9.45, give me a few minutes. I will dress up."

"Sure," Amanda whispered back, now remembering to do so.

Ananya went back to her bedroom to dress.

Amanda walked with her drink to the other bedroom, taking care not to make a sound.

This room had a baby cradle, little stuffed toys, and white walls with multicoloured polka-dotted curtains. She made a mental note of the inviting plush baby crib with soft satin-cotton American blankets in yellow, olive green, blue, and white.

'She must not be using it for Alia,' she thought, looking at the crib that was piled with baby towels and nappies. 'Ananya's home has a lot of emotion,' concluded her friend at the end of her tour, sitting on the edge of the bed.

In the other room, Alia shifted in her sleep. Ananya sat next to her in her undergarments, gingerly patting her back to sleep, and pulled up the soft bedcovers around her. Alia's little white cheeks had turned crimson, sleeping on one side for long. She observed Alia's slightly open pink lips and little drooping cheeks on the soft baby pillow for some time before getting into a formal shirt and a Lafayette New York pin stripe ankle pants.

Ananya checked herself in the long mirror of her bedroom.

She looked taller than her 5.6" height and much more tanned.

'I must have tanned at least two shades,' she wondered.

Her large ash brown eyes stared back. They looked larger with dark circles. Her little straight nose and unassumingly pouted lips stood out against her sunken cheeks.

'My face looks longer and more oval than before. Amanda was correct. I must have lost weight!' She pulled her hair in a neat bun to clip it high and pulled the black belt around her waist tightly to hold her pants.

Except for a hint of kohl in her eyes, she decided to go for a 'no make-up' look.

Alia again shifted in her sleep and whimpered slightly.

Ananya picked her baby and the bag that she had set with day's necessities and looked around one last time. Things were strewn in a mess.

'I will straighten it once I'm back,' she thought and opened the door.

"Admiring my baby's room?" she asked Amanda. "I have to still clean the house a lot. It gathers a lot of dust from the Western Express Highway," Ananya said apologetically.

"This is the problem with most women. They are always on a pleasing trip because of which they cannot move up in life."

Amanda ran her eyes on Ananya and started to whistle slowly. "You look great, darling! You have the bum of that famous Latino singer Jlow. It's literally sticking outta those pants! The job is yours, girl!" She extended a hand for Alia.

"I will not be hired for how my behind fits into my pants, dear!" Ananya said, adding, "Please take this if you can?" She extended the bag instead in her direction.

"Of course!" Amanda took the bag.

"I have kept the cough syrup, if need be," Ananya informed her.

"Don't worry! Ranjeeta will take care of everything. Besides, you will be back soon. Let's go!"

The peon walked into the cabin with the printout of a CV. Sushma Vohra, the top HR manager from Arora & Arora Ltd. was checking the mails for the day. She was a highly professional no-nonsense woman in her late thirties. One of her responsibilities included screening people coming in for top positions.

She took the CV from the peon and placed it on her table without bothering to look at it.

"Ask madam to sit," she instructed the peon.

"She is," he responded in Hindi and went out.

Sushma checked the time in her watch. It was 11.40.

The lady who had come that day for the interview was a recommendation from a very senior editor and CEO of a top publishing house in town, a friend of Arora's.

Sushma just looked at the profile papers on her desk in resignation and went about checking the mail again. The lady in question had applied for the post of the senior editor with *AFTER TEA*, their lifestyle magazine.

AFTER TEA was a lifestyle magazine published by Arora & Arora for a limited clientele to start with. A&A was in the business of interiors, stock market investments, and construction for a 100 years now. AFTER TEA was their business venture with a huge VISION—One: to reach out to the 'who's who' of the business world. Two: to make money. One and a half years into its publication, it was still unknown. It had a meagre clientele of about 2,000, of which 1,000 were just friends and well-wishers of A&A. It was almost limping to its closure.

"Ananya Bhatt, major and topper Mumbai University in English Literature, best editor of her college magazine for five consecutive years" read the profile in bold letters.

'All these people are the same. They make bombastic profiles that never match up to their performances or talent,' thought Sushma, frustrated.

#

Frustration was writ all over the face of the receptionist outside the cabin that Ananya waited. The girl was jumbling calls, overseeing the guests and the people coming in for the interviews, and attending to other mundane chores; the tasks were unending.

Ananya sat on the sofa sipping the hot ready-made coffee handed out to her by the peon opposite to the receptionist-cum-telephone operator. Ananya was taken aback at first by the girl's pink flowing kurta and maroon lipstick.

'I need to adjust to the city's fast work culture, ethics, Indian weather, and, most importantly, dressing sense,'

Ananya thought wryly. She finished her coffee and kept the cup on the side table.

"Madam, was the coffee good?" The girl in pink asked in colloquial heavily accented English in between her many jobs.

"Oh yes!" Ananya lied. "Thank you!"

She had got a file to the interview with her testimonials. The file contained her certificates and also the published work from her college, which were faded and torn in places.

'The articles are so simple,' she thought. 'No way will they match up to the standards of a magazine.' True to speak, the college magazine seemed immature. It was, at the most, a spirited venture on her part for a young crowd. The low feeling and nervousness returned. She skipped a few torn pages with shivering hands till she came to a colourful one.

The heading read—

'You can lose something that you have; you cannot lose something that you already are.'

The peon was signalling to her by now from the door.

"Madam is calling you!"

Ananya stood up. She checked the time in her mobile before switching it off. It was 11.45.

She entered a spacious cabin that was tastefully done up in wood-coloured furniture. 'This is the characteristic of the entire office,' Ananya observed. 'The earthen wooden colour is giving this place a very old-world English feel.'

Sushma Vohra had Ananya's profile in her hands when she entered. She extended a manicured hand to greet her.

"I am Sushma Vohra, head HR, A&A. Please sit down."

Ananya sat after shaking hands with the lady. Her handshake was limp, observed Sushma.

"It's a Lifestyle magazine, ma'am, as you are aware," Sushma said with forced courtesy.

Ananya nodded without speaking.

"We are looking for a person who can match up to our vision," Sushma informed her with pride.

"Yes, ma'am." There was a slight shiver in Ananya's voice.

Sushma passed her eagle gaze on Ananya's clothes. A small yellow stain on her left shoulder spoilt the white shirt that she was wearing. "I am sure you must be aware of our vision as well?" she asked with no expectation and with forced cordiality, again nodding.

"Ye . . . yes," Ananya responded.

Sushma's eyes took in the closely cut nails and the dark circles under the eyes; her sharp gaze did not miss out on the lack of confidence in Ananya's voice either, and her total lack of style was hitting on the face! To speak the least, the perfectionist and super career woman Sushma was not at all impressed. 'She has a high recommendation we cannot ignore,' she thought. Sushma decided not to ask any more questions and allow her employer to take a decision on Ananya.

Ananya opened her file. "These are some of my um . . . articles . . . um."

"It's not necessary," Sushma rejoined abruptly, looking at the old published papers without interest. She forced a smile.

"Sir is waiting to speak to you about our publication." She stood up and extended her hand, signalling an end to their meeting. "Hope to work with you soon." Her voice was bleak.

Ananya could not get up immediately as she had some of the papers in her lap. By the time she stood up, Sushma was back in her chair with a distant look in her eyes and an artificial smile.

Ananya reached the door and turned around to wish her.

"Thank you. You have a great day!"

Sushma was past listening to Ananya. She just nodded without even shifting her gaze from the computer screen in front of her.

'She is not going to get hired,' she thought. 'She cannot be competent!'

#

The peon was standing bang outside the door when Ananya came out.

He pointed towards his right and said, "Sir's cabin," without preamble.

Ananya walked towards the direction she was told. She did not have a great feeling after the HR meeting.

'She did not even bother to look at me,' she thought! 'I am far removed from the aggressive work environment. Maybe I am destined to rot in a small-time school job for a meagre salary for the rest of my life, trying to make ends meet!' Alia's sick face danced in front of her eyes. That low feeling returned. 'Why did you leave me, Rahul,' her heart cried, 'to fend for myself?'

It was a long corridor. There were a couple of cubicles on either side of it as she entered, and then the corridor extended further. At the far end, there was a large wooden door; upon reaching it, she read the name of the person she needed to meet. This cabin was segregated from the others.

She knocked softly. There was no response; she knocked again a little loudly. "Come in!" said a male voice.

Ananya walked in.

She entered a huge room with rich wooden interiors and white walls, like the rest of the offices on the floor.

A semicircular table was at the far-end right corner, facing the windows in the room. An elegant wooden sofa with cushioned bottom faced the door from where she entered. A small four-seater conference table was placed next to the sofa in the middle of the room with a hanging red study focus light. A small white writing board was mounted on the wall facing the table to the left, next to the sofa.

A man was working at the far-end table with his back turned to her. "Please take a seat. I will see you in a minute," he said without turning around.

"Sure," Ananya heard herself say.

She took a mental note of the room from where she sat. There was a red pin-up board on the wall facing her. Innumerable newspaper clippings and notices were pinned to the board. Dozens of marker pens, project designs on cardboard papers, and dusters were lying on the table along with a few issues of *AFTER TEA*. A plush wall-to-wall grey carpet adorned the floor. The large windows at the farthest end were open, unlike the other offices. Except for the focus light on the conference table, none of the lights were on. Sunlight came in profusely through the open windows.

'This guy loves natural light,' Ananya observed.

Warm ocean breeze mixed with the sounds and smells of life outside wafted in. Somehow Ananya liked this cabin. She sunk comfortably into the sofa. The man finished his work on the laptop in a minute and walked towards her.

"Sorry to have made you wait, ma'am," he said.

Ananya was expecting a middle-aged or an old gentleman; instead; she was pleasantly surprised to find a much, much younger guy here.

She stood up, and the file in her lap fell down. The papers spread on the floor. Ananya felt a stab of shame looking at the worthless old printouts again. She bent down to collect them.

"Allow me," the man said and collected them for her.

She could not but wonder at the sharp contrast of humility between the lady HR head she had just met and this young man.

"Please come this way," he said, straightening up and handing out the papers to Ananya. She followed him to his table. On reaching the table, he motioned her to sit down and extended his hand.

"I am Vicky, Vicky Arora."

"Hi," Ananya said softly. "I am Ananya, Ananya Bhatt."

Vicky was surprised at Ananya's unusual way of greeting for an interview and her easy style. He motioned her to sit. She took a chair opposite to him.

"You have got your testimonials of course?" he asked, smiling.

"Yes, yes!" she responded, immediately handing him the entire file of articles and certificates that she had brought along.

He took it from her in a quick sweep of his hand and started going through the certificates. They looked authentic. He smiled again at her. 'If all goes well, I will put her on a pay scale of 500,000 per year,' he thought. 'That should be good enough.' According to his friend, she was just starting her career.

"You are a major in English Literature? Wow! You were a topper? Great! Umm," he said brightly.

Ananya nodded without a word.

He was reading her work intently without lifting his head. His sharp nose and deep dark eyes with his thin pursed-up lips complemented his flawless auburn complexion. A muscle flexed in his arm as he turned a page. 'He must be working out,' Ananya observed and could not but wonder at his formal attire in the hot Mumbai climate.

'He is very tall,' she thought. 'Very, very tall. Maybe six feet or more, maybe, maybe not.' Now he had an expression of utter concentration and a quizzical look while reading the articles.

She thought she saw an expression of disappointment cross Vicky's face. That familiar feeling of low returned.

Time moved slowly; Ananya felt restless. She needed to go back home to her sick child. All this was taking too long; looking at these people's expressions, she was sure of not getting selected. 'So what the heck!' she thought.

Vicky was disappointed too; when his friend from the best media house had recommended Ananya, he had expected a smart young professional.

"Your articles date back to 2006, 2007, ma'am? Umm. Did you write any recently?"

'Did she write anything recently?' The mucus came to her throat.

"I, err, sir, I did not get the time as I got married. All these articles are from my college days."

"Of course! Of course!" Vicky responded with forced courtesy.

"Are you trained in soft skills? I mean apart from of course the qualification that you have?" he asked, forcing a smile again. "Like Quark Xpress or Corel Draw?"

"I, err, umm, yes." 'What were they?' Ananya's mind raced. "I, I shifted abroad with my husband, and I could not pursue these professional qualifications, sir." Ananya's voice trailed.

"I understand," rejoined Vicky. "That must not have given you any time to pursue career-related studies I understand . . . I understand, umm," Vicky repeated.

Vicky handed Ananya her file. The articles were all very basic. 'They are at least five years old and have nothing to do with the theme of my magazine,' he mused. They were about the neighbouring colleges or some kind of student issues. In short, they were useless for him.

"Have you written anything on lifestyle issues apart from these . . . these, these peppy articles of course?" he asked in an encouraging tone as a last hope.

"Lifestyle? Umm as in?" Ananya asked to make sure.

"As in people, food, restaurants, fashions, clothes, interiors. Anything and everything to do with these topics?"

"No," responded Ananya. "I never had the opportunity." Ananya found herself saying, "If I get an opportunity, I might, I might, I will." Ananya's voice trailed again.

The interview was not going anywhere.

"You just have to walk in, and the job is yours," Amanda had told her. She felt an utmost feeling of worthlessness again. She felt angry at herself for taking a chance like this. She started to fume, her gullet drying! 'Is qualification everything for a job?' she thought with a rising sense of frustration.

Vicky stood up and walked to the coffee machine near the window.

He asked, forcing a smile, "Do you want some, ma'am?"

"No, no! Thank you." Ananya busied herself putting back the papers in the folder.

He observed her from the corner of his eye.

'The industry is full of aggressive sharks,' he thought. 'She seems to be too soft and simple. Besides, she does not fit the organisational image or the vision of the product.' He needed a smart, young, peppy, and vigorous woman or a man to fill the post.

'Apart from the English Literature background and a few random publications at the graduation level, she has nothing. The post was vacant for three months now, and finding the right person from the market was not easy either,' he mused. 'Highly qualified journalists demanded a lot of salary. *AFTER TEA* was not doing very well for them to hire a professional at an exorbitant price.' Besides, Vicky did not want to lose a highly powerful friend's goodwill by rejecting Ananya outright!

He wanted to give her a chance, but on what grounds?

He sipped his coffee, thinking and looking at the far-off ocean.

His father had once said, **"There is something special in every person, Son. Don't ever underestimate anyone."**

Ananya by now felt angry, frustrated, and humiliated. All kinds of negative feelings within her were fighting to give way. It was almost two hours since she was here, and she felt trapped. The people seemed to be utterly cold and snobbish too! She waited as the gentleman who was taking her interview was sipping coffee slowly. That infuriated her further! From what she could see, he seemed interested neither in her profile nor in hiring her! So why waste time? She needed to go back! To her most precious Alia! Maybe by now she had cried herself hoarse, or possibly the maid might have left her hungry. Worse her fever might have increased! She needed to leave and immediately! She did not care any more about the interview!

'Is the Interview over?' Ananya asked. She turned to look at Vicky. "Look, sir, I cannot sit here, while you take a decision. You might as well intimate me later," she said, forcing as much of courtesy as possible in her voice.

Vicky jumped out of his thoughts.

"I, er, I . . ."

"Excuse me for saying this, sir!" Ananya's voice rose as she continued, "I really do not know how things function here in this country, but I had expected a lot more courtesy and respect for time as it's on the road to becoming a superpower!"

Vicky was observing Ananya for the first time.

'She had a slight lingering American accent, a strong voice, possibly a fiery temper,' he thought.

"Please, ma'am," Vicky started, "I do not know why you should feel this way but . . ."

She interjected, raising her voice a little, "Being a free person of the largest democratic country in the world, I take the liberty to point out that a person's dress should not come in the way of getting hired." As Ananya spoke now, she had a swing to her voice. "I mean, it should not be the only criteria!"

Vicky saw her eyes for the first time; they were large, brown, and had a peculiar fire in them that would compel people to listen to her!

He moved away from the window with an apologetic smile on his face. "Of course it should not!"

Ananya continued, "I know that beggars are no choosers, sir. I am one, sitting here, but every person does not sprout and become a great entity in a day."

Vicky nodded as he had nothing to say, wondering at her clear, immaculate language.

"Sir, you have the freedom to reject me," said Ananya, standing up and collecting her file. "Or hire me. I will not contradict that, but let me make it clear that I would not like to accept work on the basis of mercy either. I am here because of a friend who forced me, because of a friend who had great faith in my abilities. I don't know why?" Ananya's voice was crystal clear and rose above the sound of traffic coming from the windows.

'My God!' thought Vicky. 'How appearances can be deceptive!' His father was right!

"I do not think that qualifications can decide a man's merit at work," Ananya was saying. "Otherwise, so many people in our country will not be jobless, sir. Having said that, if you do not give a chance to someone to prove themselves, how will they? It's like never digging a gold mine! Anyway, thanks for your time and for collecting the worthless papers from the floor for me. I really appreciate such a humble gesture from an affluent person like you!"

She started to move.

"Please sit down," Vicky said. "Please!" He went to his side of the table. "It's a request, please?"

Ananya sat down, shivering with emotion.

Vicky said slowly, taking his time, "We will put you on a consolidated salary of 500,000 per year. You will be on probation for a period of three months. If your performance is good, then we will give an increment of 20 per cent immediately after the probation period. Is that all right with you? Please tell me if you have any further expectations right now."

Ananya's first thought was, she had just not heard it right. "You mean?"

"I mean I am hiring you not because of a recommendation but because I see a great potential in you, Ms Ananya! Will you accept this job offer?"

Ananya just looked at Vicky wide eyed. "What?"

He observed her large restless eyes, flaring nostrils, and sunken cheeks. He was not making a mistake. He knew it! He asked again, "Is 500,000 OK with you? We are paying you less because of your lack of experience, otherwise we pay more." He added clearly.

Ananya just sat there, staring at Vicky without seeing him.

He slowly passed on the small bottle of mineral water that was on the table towards her. She took a sip.

"We will mail you the appointment letter and the salary structure in a day or two. Please respond asap as we need to start work immediately!"

"Yes." It was a gentle whisper. Did she hear it right, 500,000? 'That means,' she made a quick mental calculation, '40,000 odd per month?' She would be paid more within three months if she performed well? She started for the door.

"Thank you for your time, ma'am," Vicky said. "You have a great day!"

"Thanks," said Ananya. She walked slowly to the door and closed it without looking back! She was in a daze!

Vicky met a lot of people in his life. Nobody had surprised him as much as Ananya. The fiery grey-brown eyes played in his memory long after she had left. He thought, **'She is different!'**

"The difference in servants is, some are kind and some are not! Some are truthful and honest, and some are not. We cannot do anything about it, darling! I am telling you from experience to follow gut feelings while hiring one rather than going by the impressive biodata," Amanda had told Ananya before giving her the number of the maidservant agency in Kalina, Mumbai, from where she had hired Ranjeeta herself.

Mrs Mishra and Ananya were waiting to meet a servant from Top Maidservants, an agency, at Ananya's house that afternoon. Mrs Verma had gone for a kitty party; otherwise, she was too eager to grill the servant herself.

"I cannot miss this kitty," Mrs Verma had said. "I need to see what Mrs Sharma is making for brunch today. She was too critical of my home-made *pani puri* last kitty!"

Mrs Verma wore her green chiffon sari and sleeveless blouse and ran to the kitty in the neighbourhood.

"Look at mine. She is always late. She always lies to me when I ask her for an explanation. These maids are all the same!" Mrs Mishra complained.

Ananya smiled, "Mrs Mishra, it's OK, since Kanta *bai* is not staying at your place. Now that I need to leave Alia with mine, she has to be really good."

"*Haan, haan,*" agreed Mrs Mishra. "Very important," she rejoined, swinging her head.

"I want a servant exactly like yours, Amanda, caring and good," Ananya had requested her friend.

"Its luck, baby," Amanda had rejoined. "I am lucky to find Ranjeeta. Hope the same with you."

Ananya reflected, remembering the way Ranjeeta had taken care of Alia when she was at the interview.

"What is your name?" Mrs Mishra asked the maid authoritatively.

"Marriamma."

"Marriamma? Catholic name? Where are you from?"

"I am from Kerala. I am Christian, madam."

Ananya had Marriamma's biodata. She was a mother of two boys of six and eight. She had left them in the care of her mother and sister-in-law to work in Mumbai for a livelihood. Her husband was an alcoholic and a drug addict. She had come to the city of dreams four years back and had an impressive record of caring for a toddler and a five-year-old as a full-time housemaid in Goregaon for four years. She spoke Malayali fluently, Hindi, and some broken English.

"Please sit," requested Ananya.

Marriamma sat on the carpet.

"Why did you leave the work with the previous family?" Ananya asked.

"They went to America, madam," Marriamma said. Her voice was soft, which impressed Ananya.

"Oh! OK. Was that the only house you worked in?" asked Mrs Mishra again.

"*Haan, haan.*"

Her record seemed to be clean and so did she. Her clothes and nails, Ananya observed, were very clean. She was buxom, dark, and in her late thirties. Marriamma reminded Ananya of Abilene, a black woman maid from the bestselling book *The Help* by Kathryn Stockett, which she had finished reading recently. Like Abilene, Marriamma was dark but not careworn. She had a peaceful, pleasant, smiling face with the hands of a mother. Large wide palms like palm leaves.

'She can cradle and accommodate a baby effortlessly in those palms,' thought Ananya.

"Follow your intuition," Amanda's voice reverberated in her head.

"Hmmm. We have a small baby. You will have to take care of her whole day while madam goes to work," informed Mrs Mishra in a bossy tone. Marriamma answered all their questions with a smiling face.

'She is very matured, a sign of patience,' thought Ananya.

The next moment was a decisive one. One moment they were all questioning the servant, and the next Marriamma was on her feet. Without Ananya's knowledge, Alia was choking on something.

Marriamma sprang like lightning and held the baby in her large hands straight, facing her. She manoeuvred a finger into Alia's little mouth. Alia coughed up a small hard plastic colourful rubber cube that she had put in.

"It could have choked her," Ananya cried snatching Alia from Marriamma's hands. Everything happened within seconds.

Ananya hired Marriamma on the spot.

"I will teach you everything about my home, baby, and how to go about the work for fifteen days before confirming you? Can you join from tomorrow? I need someone urgently." Marriamma nodded. She had no objection.

'That will also give me the opportunity to observe her', Ananya thought, 'before joining A&A.'

Book II

SPRING

After Three Months

"Before joining **AFTER TEA**, were you with a lifestyle magazine?"

"No."

"Which publication did you work with before to this?"

"None."

There was a commotion amongst the journalists. Quizzical expressions were exchanged; some laughed in subdued tones.

"With no finance, as **AFTER TEA** is obviously not doing well, and no experience to boot, how will you fight the big names in the market?" asked a journalist.

"Forget about fighting, who will even look at your publication, madam?" another shouted.

The relaunch was Ananya's idea, but handling erratic journalists was another. She looked around with trepidation. She was heading the press conference along with her team. Her face went red. She was far from prepared for this kind of grilling.

'Were not all press conferences about talking, listening, taking notes, and writing bombastic reviews?' She had a wrong idea then.

Ananya spoke into the mike in a shivering tone. "Everyone present here must know that I do not want to compete with anyone." There was uproar in the room. She continued, "First, I want to bring about a refreshing change in the product by improving its quality, secondly retaining our current customers will be worked on!" She fumbled with the pen in her hand nervously. "Once these things are in place, I . . . I . . . I am also working on the strategies for better marketing, distribution, and circulation."

There was a lot of noise as nobody was listening.

"Well, after this relaunch, I am sure . . ." She paused. Raising her voice uncertainly, she continued, "We will increase our clientele with the help of the press." She smiled nervously, looking around for support.

"It is a general rumour that because **AFTER TEA** was almost closing, the organisation hired you as they could not afford a professional. Is that true, madam?" asked a lady journalist while others laughed.

"Are you making castles in the air, with no experience and all these strategies?" asked another. They were tearing her apart! What was she to do?

"I, I, umm . . ." She fumbled for words. She found none.

Her technical support, Nilesh, came to her rescue. "Please do not ask personal questions to madam. We are proud of her," he said in faltering English.
"Our organisation, umm, and we have full faith in her."

Ananya's heart went out to her team members, who were as nervous as she was. They were a bunch of young people with little qualification and blind faith in an inexperienced person like her.

She took several deep breaths, her face went red out of fear, and she clasped the pen more tightly for support, before speaking out, as her legs trembled under the table.

"I am challenging, I am promising," she corrected herself. "Any big-time lifestyle magazine will get competition and a run for its money and popularity a year from now."
Several eyebrows escaped into hairlines.

"Is she kidding?" she heard someone smirk.

"*AFTER TEA . . .*" Ananya faltered, struggling for words. "*AFTER TEA, AFTER TEA . . .*"

"Please speak further," a journalist shouted, laughing as several followed suit.

"Will be one of the best lifestyle magazines in business, I promise, gentlemen!" Ananya surprised herself.

There was silence as the press took some time to process her statement.

"I will not leave any stone unturned to actualise, to actualise that dream," she finally concluded. The pens got busy.

"Yes! Yes!" rejoined Richa, the subeditor. "I support and endorse ma'am's statement." She punched the thin air with her fist.

"I am sure!" said Manish, the advertising guy. "I am with you!"

"I believe!" said Nilesh. "I will work hard towards it!"

In that moment of impulse, they joined hands together. They pulled Ananya's shaking hand and put it on top of theirs!

"What a team spirit," blurted out a critical woman journalist in giggles.

The flashlights came full on them.

"I will throw the same statement at her after a year, you will see," remarked another female laughing.

"If this publication still exists," added another male friend of hers, guffawing.

"A bunch of losers," someone remarked under his breath.

"They sure have guts to challenge the best," a third man said. The women around him giggled in ridicule. At the end, they all thought, 'Anyways, we had a good time at the expense of that scared, shivering woman.'

A few more erratic questions and the relaunch press conference ended with the amused journalists dispersing.

#

After the fiery question-answer session with the press, Ananya was walking in the long corridor to her cubicle, followed by her team members.

The whole office of A&A that occupied the first two floors of an industrial estate in Oshiwara was divided into separate sections dedicated to different departments, like real estate, finance, interiors, in that order. A first-floor wing was dedicated to **AFTER TEA**. The team worked from the cubicles which were clustered together, while Ananya had her own separate cabin adjacent to them. The conference hall was on the ground floor.

Ananya's face had a unique glow; her eyes were focused, her shoulders straight. She held her head high, trying not to show her feelings of humiliation to her team, lest they be discouraged.

"Every issue from now should answer the questions of our readers and solve their lifestyle problems. Every magazine of ours should be live, palpable, and interactive," Ananya said, looking at Richa.

Richa nodded, searching Ananya's face sympathetically for any signs of humiliation. She was running along with her, matching Ananya's steps, followed by Nilesh and Manish.

"This issue I find very different, ma'am, all about diet and health and figure," Nilesh said, encouraging Ananya.

"Fitness," Ananya corrected him, moving her head amusedly. "Not figure!" She crossed a pillar, taking a turn to the staircase; all did the same. "Did you, by any chance, get the time to take the printouts for proofreading, dear?" she addressed Richa again.

"Yes, ma'am. They are on your table—all the printouts of researched articles on how food can cure several illnesses, plus live supporting interviews of patients who were cured before. Interviews of the founder Mr Nair (Food Healing Centre, Andheri) along with natural healing centre Pondicherry, fitness gurus in town and several starlets practising food therapies. Oh! Yes, ma'am," she said, remembering, "I have added one Prita Narvekar's interview too, to the bunch."

"The celebrity dietitian of Bollywood actress Sameira?" asked Nilesh excitedly.

"Exactly," rejoined Richa.

"Actually," Richa spoke apologetically, "I got Prita's number from one of my neighbours yesterday, who happens to be her client. I could not contain myself and took her interview! I felt that it will add more mileage and glamour to our publication."

"That's great! You always think out of the box," added Ananya, patting Richa on her shoulder as they took the first of the steps.

"Sorry for not asking, ma'am."

"Never say that," added Ananya, smiling. In a few months, her team was totally besotted by Ananya's quick-decision-making skills, easy demeanour, and impressive personality with a slight foreign influence.

Ananya almost jumped two steps at a time. Her team did the same after her.

Nilesh was speaking. "Ma'am! I have also kept the printouts of the advertisements for the inner cover page and outer cover along with a few others that you had approved. Ma'am . . ." He paused. "At least a hundred advertisements have come," he said to lift her spirits again.

"Wow! But we will not be using all, and why did you give the printouts? Only a soft copy could have been sufficient," she said, taking deep breaths as she tackled the steps.

"Did you get the payments, Nilesh?"

"Yes, ma'am, for all."

"Good," said Ananya. Decisively she continued, "We will push some advertisements for the later issues if they are not suitable for this."

Manish interjected, "Ma'am, actually, I forgot to mention that there was a request from Mr Carpenter for more issues of the previous publication."

Now they were at the top of the stairs.

"Mr Carpenter from the previous issue?" Ananya's eyebrows came together.

"He wants to distribute some copies amongst his friends, or so he said to me."

"Oh yes! Yes, now I remember. His interview was a part of that issue, wasn't it?" Manish nodded. Suddenly Ananya had an idea. "Ask him for the number of copies required and quote double the price for these extra issues. We need all the funds in the world."

They all agreed. By now they came to the first floor!

"Manish?" Ananya turned to him as she walked.

"Mail every client of ours the revised rate card, the revised yearly packages, and ask them for more leads.

Give them a 20 per cent discount on ten issues, with 1 voucher of Rs five hundred from 'Lifestyle Store' per copy as decided earlier."

"I have already done that!" Manish informed her.

"Added to that, collect as many names as possible of owners of big restaurants, hotels, spas, interior houses, builders, and anyone and everyone in the financial sector, housing sector, hospitality, and don't forget to mail them the dummy copies of our forthcoming issue as well!"

"I have already done that, ma'am," Manish said again. "I have spoken to at least 500 more prospective clients and doing more every day. I have also put the promos of our forthcoming issue on YouTube. I have already started getting calls."

"Great! Please attend to all the calls personally. If you cannot, pass them on to me. Give them my mobile number so that I am accessible too," advised Ananya.

"Give mine too," added Richa enthusiastically.

"If ma'am and you guys can, I can also talk to people," rejoined Nilesh.

"Why not?" Ananya said. "You are a good speaker."

Nilesh's face widened in a grin. He nodded, feeling great!

By now they had reached Ananya's cabin. She opened the door to enter and stopped.

"Manish! Don't forget about the hoardings and TV ads for the forthcoming issue!"

"Ma'am." Manish hesitated.

"Yes?"

"Ma'am, I had posted our promos on WhatsApp on my mobile to a business group."

Ananya opened her mouth to protest.

"Ma'am, I have some orders after that. Thirty, and more will follow, I am sure."

"Good job, Manish. I could never think of it myself!" Ananya smiled. Manish loved to see Ananya smile. He was her ardent admirer. He hesitated before speaking again.

"Ma'am, please do not feel bad about the press conference today." He was scanning her face. Richa and Nilesh were nodding too "Press is always like that. We will show them what we can do."

"No, I am not afraid," Ananya said, lowering her gaze to hide a sudden expression of humiliation. Her team looked on with sympathy.

She almost moved into her cabin and turned back with a hand on the knob, her face expressionless the very next moment. "Thanks, Nilesh, for saving me today !"

Nilesh gave a thumbs up. "Anything for you." Ananya walked into the cabin. The nameplate on it read **Ms Ananya Bhatt—Chief Editor** *AFTER TEA*.

As the others left for lunch, she thought as she moved further in, 'I should be worth it!'

#

Ananya moved into her glass cabin that was large, meagrely furnished, and airy. She liked it that way. The colour of the furniture was light wood and beige. There was a large glass table at the furthest wall facing the door. Four rolling beige swivel chairs were around the table and one at the head. A small sofa occupied a left-hand corner. There was a pin-up board full of her plans for the forthcoming issues, growth chart for the next six months, and a couple of previous covers of ***AFTER TEA***. A dummy of the forthcoming issue without the cover picture and tentative headlines was pinned too.

After the hectic relaunch conference, Ananya was fagged out. She slumped into her chair.

She threw a glance on the pinned-up growth plan. It was charted to follow a market strategy, advertising, and distribution plan for the next six months, based on the existing market study. In the last two months, she had been able to retain the existing customers, which was an achievement in itself!

Ananya adjusted herself on the chair with an eye on the chart.

She understood by now that to have an edge over the other publications, it was not enough to follow a plan. **AFTER TEA** needed to be a live, thriving example of excellence! It needed to connect! Real stories, real people, and simple language could only bridge the gap with her readers. Her calling was to address them directly, give a solution to their lifestyle issues, and in the process, ignite a connect that could start the spurt of sales. Once it happened, there would be no stopping the wildfire!

Slowly she took a sip from the glass of water on her table and closed her eyes. She had immense belief in the spirit of Indians and word-of-mouth publicity.

'**I have to touch the hearts of my readers first. Yes, I have to,**' she told herself. '**There lies the success!**'

She read the bold words in red marker on a chart paper pinned to the board a zillionth time. They were

Truth! Simplicity! Success!

The three most 'powerful words' she had arrived at after days and days of painstaking study of the previous issues of AFTER TEA upon her immediate joining it! Ananya closed her eyes; exhausted, she sat motionless, willing, driving, propelling her mind to think 'out of the box' into feverish action. One of the things that worked surprisingly for her was reliving the bad experience of going through the previous limp

issues of the magazine. Presently, to fire up, she went back **to her little research.**

"Research is the way to invention" had read a bombastic headline . . . A blonde model in a sports bra, boobs protruding with muscles like a man, and a tennis racket in hand, stared at her from one of the old covers . . . Ananya's jaw dropped. The topic was about how women can work for a great muscled body!

'Did women like muscled bodies at all?' Ananya hated the very thought of it. She could not relate to the picture or to the woman or to the feature.

'Will an Indian woman relate to this blond bimbo?

'Never!' was her honest reply to herself.

The headline, the language, and everything about the issue was very, very irrelevant and impersonal, and a reader learnt nothing!

The other issues were equally boring. The cover pictures did not pamper her senses, and the headlines? They just dried her imagination.

The entire month of September Ananya squatted on the dry, dusty, carpeted floor of the somewhat tiny six-by-eight underground room, bereft of any furniture, except for a cupboard (which served as a library for the old issues) and a dim light for company, reading issue after issue of **AFTER TEA**. While she made extensive plans upstairs in her cabin to improvise the magazine. After-work hours were spent in the dusty basement, reading the articles—sometimes in the light from her mobile when the electric bulb was insufficient. Her face only fell and shoulders slumped at the inauthentic, stupid stories on topics like sports cars, how an electric wire can be fitted into a tube light, the latest invention of bulbs (as a side story for chandeliers), wood used worldwide for furniture, latest workout machinery, food in America as a revolution for a slim body (irrelevant to the Indian scenario), and why women like to imitate men—to speak of a few! Feelings of utter helpless hopelessness mounted in her, making her only aware of the huge responsibility she was carrying on her slender shoulders. In all honesty, she knew that this was the 'beginning of a beginning'.

Nobody had asked her to do this. If she wished, she could have decided to work as she willed, charting out plans for the future, without looking back; but the kind of person she was, she always believed in working from 'inside out'! Finally, at the end of the painful 'reading month', she jotted notes on her little pad—needs authenticity, live articles, and interviews; change language; work on the marketing, catchy headlines; overhaul of look and feel—the list was endless.

Finally, she sat digging into the inner meanings of the words that she had painstakingly zeroed on, thinking more and more deeply, further simplifying, modifying, working around the corners, searching for her own 'mantra' to reinvent. After days and hours of hard work it was revealed! It was not a huge strategy to manipulate sales or dirty market politics with competitors. To turn her dwindling publication around, she needed just three simple rules to work by; they were actually three words !

TRUTH, SIMPLICITY, SUCCESS. Ananya sat there on the floor at the end of her 'study journey', 'blinking and blank'. She had just learnt her first lessons in writing—'**Big success follows small steps, simple words can express profound meanings.**' She stared at the little pad, fighting tears.

The printouts of the articles and a few important advertisements of pivotal pages stared back at her now from her table. Though the feverish peppiness was revived in her mind, hunger pangs renewed in her stomach!

'Let me first dig into my lunch box,' she thought.

After five minutes, she was biting into her home-made chappatti roll and going through the printouts.

Her computer was on, and Alia's picture was on her screen.

'She must be sleeping now!'

Her memory of the cherubic face brought a smile, softening it a little. She took another bite of the roll, wondering at its fabulous taste.

'Marriamma cooks such good food,' she mused. 'She can manage all types of dishes. I am really lucky. She has become a part of my family so fast.'

A picture to her right had Rahul, Alia, and she smiling through the frame. It was at the San Diego zoo that they had visited with Alia on a weekend in the United States.

She put a finger gingerly on his picture for a second, caressing it! All the original feelings came back. Though she still felt lonely, she was not frequented by that low feeling so often now; instead, it was superimposed with nervousness of work pressures and worries about Alia. She skipped through the pages on her table, scanning them carefully! First, she needed to allocate and calculate the number of pages per story.

'The main story on diet healing will take ten pages with pictures . . . ' she mused. 'Hmm, with advertisements, supported with interviews, umm up to twenty.' That done, she put the printouts of the main story aside.

'The second story with all the interviews on fitness will be . . . it will be . . . umm around . . . let us see, another fifteen pages? Fine,' she thought.

'So that comes to thirty-five in total, then smaller interviews again, hmm . . . everything . . . put together fifteen more pages?' Now she glanced through the advertisements . . . separated the spa fitness centres and hotels according to the beat. 'Why not increase the number of pages for this publication? We have got a lot of advertisements this time, and the stories are very interesting! I will increase the pages to 100 then,' she told herself.

She finished her chapatti roll, took another in her left hand, and browsed . . . through the printouts, meticulously.

Swiftly, she decided the advertisements for inside, outside, and for the front inside facing page.

'Hmm.' She came to the printout of the cover picture in the end.

'The models look fake!' She made a mental note. 'I will speak to Richa about it!'

She started proofreading with the original copy on her computer screen. She read and reread the words till they jumped in front of her. She was satisfied. 'They look good but need more work for effect!' she thought.

Last was Prita's interview page. She had no copy of it on her machine, as it was a new story.

'I will just check this lady's history first.'

She googled Prita Narvekar. Presto! A whole page flashed different articles on the woman . 'She is famous! She is famous,' Ananya repeated to herself as she read the reports in awe.

'It was the month of March 2012 when a small-time dietitian Prita Narvekar came into the limelight. It was after the song "Ishara Ishara" had become a huge rage . . . with the girl in it with a

negligible waistline!' Ananya blinked and read another story.

'Right Food was a medium-sized diet consultancy office in the heart of Mumbai . . . run by Prita Narvekar . . . it was unknown for a long time but for Sameira's zero figure that came into focus . . . Prita was a star overnight.' Ananya gulped.

Another read, **'Sameira's giant posters in the famous song from the film *Ishara* was a huge hit, less because of its melody and more so for the size zero girl in it . . . in semi-nude costumes. It was all because of Prita Narvekar who . . . '** At this point Ananya lost interest and discontinued reading.

There were more reports on protests by women's organisations on women with size zero figures . . . **'Today . . . the women's organisations were crying hoarse on nudity . . . parents are worried about their daughters . . . going on crash diets . . . Girls are trying to lose weight desperately lest they lose their boyfriends to zero size girls. It's all because of Sameira's zero size and Prita Narvekar,'** read the report.

Ananya sighed; she quickly went through Prita's interview. She pursed her lips. 'My publication should be real, answering questions of real people, not some fitness plans for fancy models.'

Ananya called Richa.

"Please SMS me Ms Prita's number and the name of her consultancy. Will she be available now?" she asked.

"Yes, I think so." Without asking further questions, Richa forwarded Prita's number and the name of her diet consultancy Right Food.

'I wonder if the lady in question will be available now,' Ananya thought, dialling Prita's number. It is four in the afternoon.

#

It was four in the afternoon, and a figure walked into Right Food in a hot miniskirt and a bustier; most of her midriff was exposed, leaving very little to the imagination. She was accompanied by two muscular men looking around suspiciously.

"Her bodyguards!" a lady in the clinic whispered.

The receptionist stood up nervously.

"I have an appointment for four o'clock!" said the half-clad woman with a false American accent.

"Yes, yes, this way. Prita ma'am is waiting for you."

A hush, hush silence fell in the office as the half-clad girl passed, leaving a heavy perfume behind her in the air. It was that time of the day when men were mostly working and women were free.

"Is she an actress?" asked one woman who was waiting for her turn.

"Yes, I think so," said another.

"She is that starlet, the item number," said a third.

"Oh, ya, ya, now I recognise her, eerrr . . . her name is . . . let me think . . . I forgot . . . what is it?" said the first.

"Rashi Ahuja," informed the receptionist proudly.

"Oh God, that Rashi? She is sooo cheap! A strip-goddess!" another woman whispered.

"How ugly she looks," said her friend. "She was on the cover of *Starbust* magazine this month, imagine. Did you see all those pouting lips and all?" The other woman moved her head in ridicule.

"So ugly these starlets," said another gossiping aunty. "How they come on the covers of such famous magazines?"

"Yes, they are ever ready! Casting couch. My God! We are from decent families, *baba*. We cannot do such things."

"She is sooooo skinny! Such a skinny girl having such big boobs, attracting attention of men, cheappo. They must be fake." They made dirty faces.

"Of course, silicon *ka kamal hai*" (it is all silicon), said the second.

"Because of these people, we have to also take care of our figures. My husband is gone crazy. He wants a slim figure for me. Is it possible or what, tell me, at this age?" asked the aunty, agitated.

All the women sighed in agreement.

After about half an hour, the skinny figure with protruding boobs came out. All women made faces, exchanging glances.

A child accompanied by a toddler in his care ran towards the starlet. The toddler pulled at Rashi's skirt and put his head between her legs while the seven-year-old stood like a statue, holding his brother's hand eyeing her booties.

Rashi started screaming, "I hate this! I hate! Someone please take these kids away. I hate kids. Please save me." Turning angrily towards the receptionist, she said, "I am sorry I do not have time for autographs. Please tell the people here not to bother me again!"

The kids' mom ran and rescued her children from the screaming 'bootilicious witch'.

Prita almost came out of her little cabin. The receptionist sprang to her feet, shaking.

The whole commotion lasted a few seconds, and the bodyguards whisked the starlet away. Prita's clinic experienced such hyper incidents frequently nowadays. In fact, she looked forward to such commotions which increased her popularity without wasting money and attracted clientele like 'bees to honey'!

"What attitude! Who wants her autograph anyway?" said the fat aunty. "Who knows her? Whore!"

"But she smells good," said the third besotted woman.

"Hope the press asks for my interview!" All looked at the mother with jealousy.

"You should not take your kids everywhere!" complained the aunty.

"Where do I leave them for an hour in the afternoon? Don't you people watch *Crime Patrol*?" said the almost-famous mom.

Prita went back into her little cabin quietly with a smug smile. She could vouch for at least a month's hike in business after the mad incident!

As she moved in . . . Prita's phone on her desk rang.

"Hi, this is Prita Narvekar's Right Food consultancy," she responded with the artificial sweetness she had so sincerely practised after Sameira's size zero hype.

"Hi, ma'am" Ananya said into the mouthpiece. "I am Ananya, chief editor *AFTER TEA* magazine, um . . . Richa, my subeditor, had taken your interview yesterday?"

"Oh! Yes, yes! I remember! How are you? Hope you found my answers usable?" Prita responded in her characteristic stylish, sweet tone.

"Is it a good time to talk to you?" Ananya asked.

"Yes, please go ahead," Prita responded, adding, "Excuse me for a minute."

Ananya could overhear her speak to someone on the intercom. "Don't send in Mrs Kumar for another fifteen minutes, please. I am on a call."

"Sorry, ma'am, please continue." Prita came back on the line.

Ananya spoke slowly and sweetly (a trait that she had discovered about herself and which worked with people),

"Prita, I am sorry to disturb you, but I still have a few questions to ask."

"The pleasure is all mine," Prita responded in her sugar-coated tongue again.

For the next fifteen minutes, Ananya spoke to Prita about diet dos and don'ts and the urban Indian's dilemma on eating right.

"Prita, in our country at least 70 to 80 per cent of people eat rice. What will be your advice to them? There seems to be a lot of confusion regarding dieting and rice eating."

"In truth, rice is good for digestion. It prevents ageing and is nutritious for even diabetics. It has all the vital vitamins needed by our body." Prita went on for the next ten minutes about the goodness of rice.

Ananya took notes hungrily.

After a while, she said, "It is always wise to decide the portions to keep your weight in check. Brown rice is always better than the plain white rice, one must remember."

"Thank you so much! It was really, really, very insightful," Ananya said and added, "I am dying to know how Sameira became size zero."

With Sameira's mention, there was immediate enthusiasm in Prita's voice.

"With her own dedication and hard work of course," she laughed, the artificial sweetness returning back. "Sameira is a good student. I am proud to be her dietitian." She wound up mysteriously, adding for effect, "If you'll please excuse me, I have a few clients waiting. It was great talking to you. You can follow my blogs on twitter for the latest in the world of diet and fitness." She hung up!

Ananya reflected, 'She really deserves to be a celebrity nutritionist. I am going to follow a diet plan too, to lose this.' She ran a soft hand quickly over her own baby bump. She reframed several lines from her notes. The articles needed some more editing for perfection! With the present issue, Ananya was hoping some success for her magazine. This was the third issue after she had joined. As luck would have it, they had some amazing articles and interviews to boot. She checked the time; it was five o'clock. 'I will have coffee and finish with rest of the writing!' She walked to the cafeteria on the fourth floor.

#

Vicky was on the first floor that day, checking on some ongoing projects. He had decided to work from his Oshiwara office. He was moving to the ground floor from the first, when he saw Ananya move past him in the corridor without noticing him. She looked more confident compared to a forlorn nervous lady he had met some months back. Vicky kept a tab on all his employees inside out without their knowledge. He was carefully following up on *AFTER TEA's* progress and Ananya. He felt happy for her.

Vicky went ahead to the ground floor where his car was parked.

Ananya felt happy when she went to the cafeteria. Richa and Nilesh were already there joking, laughing, kicking each other. They were drinking ready-made coffee from paper cups and reading Chinese predictions on them.

"You will be angry at someone today," read Nilesh on his cup.

Richa went into peals of laughter. "You did, on the journalists, today."

Ananya could not help but smile broadly.

"You will not win a fight today!" Richa read hers next.

"See, see, it's against me," rejoined Nilesh. Richa showed him a mock fist, and all of them laughed.

"I wonder how these predictions are so true," Ananya wondered aloud.

"What is yours, ma'am?" asked Richa and Nilesh at the same time.

Ananya read hers . . . "Something will inspire you today." All of them chatted around the little table, drinking coffee happily for some time afterwards.

#

Ananya returned to her cabin after a while, feeling refreshed and lite. The Herculean task of putting the entire issue together still remained. She stood in front of the pin-up board, absently staring at the plans.

Her mind suddenly flew back in time to a similar situation, to a day, in college, when she was standing in front of the noticeboard, reading an article. She was in the first year of graduation and had won the first prize in an inter-collegiate competition for feature writing.

"Who is this Ananya?" a student exclaimed to another . . . "Her article has won first prize."

The other agreed, "Very interesting . . ."

"It's all about dating, yaar," said the third.

"Very, very interesting!" It was Professor Mrs Manjula, who had stopped by to glance at the board too . . . "She is my student of Literature," she announced to the others proudly.

The students nodded obediently, exchanged glances, and stifled giggles . . . at the sight of the snobbish professor.

Mrs Manjula was the English and journalism professor for the entire college and worked as a photo-journalist in her spare time.

Ananya came forward. "Ma'am, I am here." Mrs Manjula adjusted her spectacles on her tiny nose and patted Ananya on the shoulder.

"Good style, my dear girl. I am very proud of you . . . the article violates grammar rules though . . ." Ananya bit her tongue while the professor continued, "But good. Like Ernest Hemingway . . . no grammar rules! Conversational but concise." On that note Mrs Manjula walked away into the staff room joined by another colleague, discussing some student issues.

Ananya turned around to bump into Shourya, their college football champion, who was also reading the noticeboard.

"Hey, congo . . . good arti . . . Good style, my dear girl," he said, copying Mrs Manjula's words, mocking Ananya!

"Thanks."

They started to walk. Shourya walked along, brushing Ananya's hand with his. She remembered him having the notorious reputation of a serial kisser who chased every skirt or imaginable female dress on the campus, and naturally, 'decent girls' maintained a distance from him.

Ananya went to her table, smiling; she recollected the day very vividly. She took a writing pad and noted the words—natural good style, simple language, conversational, and . . . and concise . . . ummm . . . 'concise' . . . means—'short'.

She went back in memory again, trying to remember . . . the incident clearly.

She recollected that they had walked to the college grounds next, where Veer (their college cricket captain) was practising with the team. Tall, handsome, with razor-sharp features, a second-year journalism student, Veer always used to win trophies for their college in cricket. Ananya had a huge crush on him. He was her all-time favourite. As they neared the ground, he shouted, perspiration running to his toes.

"Hey, Ananya! Congo! Great work, buddy! Nice article!"

"What do you like about it?" Ananya screamed.

"Right for a college crowd. Powerful . . . Inspiring! I could connect."

Ananya noted down . . . powerful, inspiring, connecting.

"Still, what do you like about it?"

"Dating . . . simple . . . how to bunk lectures and go to a theatre with your girl . . . or to CCD . . . not get caught," rejoined Shourya, laughing from her side.

"Shut up, Shourya! Tell me, Veer?"

"It's very compelling, man . . . not boring . . . not at all. Congo again."

Ananya wrote the words—compelling, entertaining, understand the audience . . . She jerked back. 'From here on, *AFTER TEA* will include stories with all the above factors . . . I know how to work on them now!' Motivated by herself, she went ahead writing the editors note:

In the world of food, health, and nutrition, it's sometimes hard to separate fact from fiction. This month, we uncover the unknown facts about eliminating nutritional deficiencies, about achieving size zero figures and flat tummies by just eating right! For the first time, doctors in business open up about the importance of making friendship with food to escape costly, dangerous procedures like liposuction and to allow food to start the process of slimming! We have story after story that tells you the unknown and unread facts about how to indulge your taste buds and lose weight! These are real people with their success

stories about 'diet healing'! To add to all this, we have the celebrated nutritionist Ms Prita Narvekar's most candid and inspirational interview about 'Eat to reduce your waist line!' For the first time ever, Ms Prita reveals to all us Indians the importance of consuming rice as a staple diet plan! Actress Sameira Khan's zero figure facts and more . . .

Diwali was round the corner, so Ananya closed the note with

' . . . wishing all our readers A Very Happy Diwali!'
Only, she did not know then that the issue would create a furore.

At the end of the day, Ananya saved all the edited articles with the editor's note in one folder on her desktop for final designing by Nilesh. Only the cover needed to be shot, and it was scheduled for the next day!

#

Next day, Ananya was at Shatranj Napoli, 2 Union Park, Pali Hill, Khar, Mumbai.

She took a taxi and landed in the restaurant at half past one. It was a high-end Italian restaurant, 'the address' in town, frequented by the superstars like Shah Rukh Khan. It was chosen for the shoot for its ambience that was a mix of Indian and Italian, just right for Ananya's vision for the cover of the upcoming diet issue.

She stepped into Polpo Up, the private party room where the photo shoot was scheduled. One of the Bollywood's new music releases was playing in the background, and the whole place was alive with light men, a couple of designers walking with clothes on hangers, spot boys, food stylists, and hair dressers. Nilesh was present too; he was in front of the monitor to help coordinate the look that they had decided earlier. Ananya could tell that he was feeling ill at ease in such a set-up! She walked in, and he gave her a wide welcoming smile with relief! She realised at that moment how the small crew of **AFTER TEA** was fast becoming an extended family for her! The entire shoot was coordinated by Richa expertly, though she was not around that day!

Ace lensman Digmanshu sen greeted Ananya with respect. A spot boy dragged a chair for her in front of the monitor. She was handed a cup of piping hot coffee in a delicate china by another. She was asked if she had breakfast by one of the hotel staff. Ananya was impressed.

Digmanshu was in his late thirties and an amazing photographer; he was lately into making TV soaps. He was considered as one of the best in business! He was saying, "The models are almost ready. I understand that you want an Indo-Western look for a diet special issue targeted at urban Mumbaikars."

"Yes."

Ananya saw a model in Anarkali with a small diamond butterfly clip in her long hair with minimal make-up and jewellery, sitting in a corner. She was beautiful and wholesome; every inch matched the image Ananya had for the cover. She observed that she was sweet, quiet, and courteous to the people around.

"We have two models . . . don't we?"

"Yes! Tina is getting ready . . . Trisha is here already!"

"She looks perfect," added Ananya, admiring her.

Trisha was an upcoming television artist in her early twenties. She nodded quietly from her corner at Ananya. Ananya reciprocated.

A variety of foods were on the table from Indian and Italian to a spread of fruits and salads. The food stylists were constantly fussing over the spread with paint brushes. "It is all artificial. They are painting it to bring out the colour," said Digmanshu.

Nilesh moved his head in disbelief at Ananya's expression.

Tina came in a short yellow jumpsuit with front buttons open. Her artificial boobs bounced like rubber balls. She profusely flirted with the men around. The whole place held a different energy after her entry. She was tall, leggy, with satiny skin like a snake. She walked straight up to Digmanshu and pecked him on the cheek with boobs all over him.

"How do I look, darling?"

"You look gorg."

Nobody seemed to mind it!

Ananya just nodded, trying to keep her expression neutral.

"Is the look OK, madam?" asked the photographer, more out of courtesy than anything else.

"I am thinking about the dress, Digmanshu."

"OK?"

"I wanted a happening, Western, day-to-day, upmarket, fun look for the cover, not an out and out raunchy one."

Digmanshu signalled to Tina and the dress designers.

Tina came; she was watching Ananya with eagle eyes.

The designers came with dresses on hangers and some sandals. Trisha went back to her corner, looking a little upset. The hairstylist started fussing over her, mumbling something.

Trisha made a face at Digmanshu, but it was so fleeting that Ananya could not tell if she had seen it. She selected an olive green one-shoulder full-length jumpsuit with self-coloured smocking work on the waist and glass stilettos with double rhinestone straps for Tina.

What followed was most unexpected.

Tina simply slipped out of the dress she was wearing and got into the suit in everyone's presence. She had nothing on but a double-padded push-up strapless bra and a black thong underneath.

Nilesh hid his face behind the monitor while someone whispered excitedly, "She was a pin-up model for a famous swimwear brand."

"OK, madam?" she asked Ananya before going to the table to pose.

"Yes! Yes!" said Ananya, flabbergasted, but hiding her feelings.

Nobody seemed to mind it at all. Tina started to receive more respect after that.

Why not? she had the right attitude for high-fashion modelling.

Ananya just had to give it to the professionalism of the girl, though.

Digmanshu said, "She is going to make it big. You will see." I am going to cast her in the TV soap that I am making.

"Who? Tina?" Ananya asked.

"No, Trisha! She looks so innocent, so vulnerable, just like an Indian *bahu*!"

'What double standards? Why do men always want to rescue women?' Ananya thought.

Digmanshu shouted, "Smile, girls, take!"

Tina perched herself up on the side of the oval top, partially holding an artificial cherry between her juicy lips provocatively. Trisha took her position, standing with a plate of sprouted salad at the centre, next to Tina. The food stylist touched up the salad one last time while the make-up artist powdered the noses of the girls. The two light men perched on top of the ladders on each side of the table, focusing their lights.

Suddenly, the light boy on Tina's side slightly turned the light at an angle, and her cleavage was clearly visible; it moved a little as she posed, and the take was okayed. The light boys exchanged glances and winked at each other.

Obviously, the men were enjoying the shoot and the half-clad model.

All through the shoot, Ananya mustered superhuman strength to keep her expression under check as one moment was never the same as the next with Tina around. The shoot was finally over. Ananya picked five pictures for editorials and the best one for the cover from the lot. Nilesh made a note. She walked out to the entrance of the restaurant at around five to wait for the taxi that was going to pick her.

A Honda City drove past. In the back seat was Digmanshu sen. There was a woman next to him. As the car took a curve from the cobbled path into the traffic, Ananya saw Trisha lock lips with the photographer. Indeed, appearances were deceptive!

In the world of glamour, people needed to look good and act dirty but in the world of journalism according to Ananya, one needed to be talented, truthful, direct, creative, and also tactful! After returning home from the photo shoot, she was dog-tired, but her mind was working overtime. *AFTER TEA* needed hoards of publicity to stand out! Ananya's challenge was to squeeze out the maximum at minimum cost! How was she to do it?

She squatted on the carpet, wearing pyjamas after a shower, feeding little Alia home-made porridge. Ananya had to find day in day out some tricks to coax the healthy porridge of grains down Alia's mouth!

"I will read Micky. Mama will read Micky Mouse? OK? Micky? Micky? Big ears Micky?" She mimicked playfully, coaxing Alia to eat a little porridge.

Alia started to clap excitedly but twisted her face away. As a last resort, Ananya played a cartoon film, and Alia ate her food fast! It was always some kind of barter with Alia that Ananya had to work on to make her eat.

At that moment, an idea struck her. Large, small, and medium-sized magazines could advertise *AFTER TEA* free of cost or for very little. In return, Ananya and her team would promote their magazines to her clients! It would save money for the hoardings. She worked on the strategy of PLAY TO PLAY instead of PAY TO PLAY! Without her knowing it, she had adopted a method called cross-media promotion, very popular in the publishing industry. She also incorporated the judicious use of new media—Blogs, Twitter, Facebook, and LinkedIn—to establish effective marketing and business development for free. Not only that, she agreed to advertise the lifestyle outlets in town, for a minimal cost with *AFTER TEA*. In return her clients got free vouchers from the stores. The idea 'hit the nail on the head'. Preceding which she went into a long tie-up with small and medium sized stores in town. With gaining momentum, *AFTER TEA* started circulating in the high end lifestyle stores in town, within no time. It was not easy. Her consistent persistence, meticulous eye for detail, every single day, along with the support of her team gave fruit.

She met deadlines without fail. Worked on new ideas of presenting stories! Her intrinsic knowledge of English helped bring in that much-needed extra edge to the features. Ananya's natural creative demeanour, which was untapped so far, came alive! She was gaining confidence slowly and so was her team in her leadership! With three issues of *AFTER-TEA* behind her, she was able to hold her own in her conversations generally and in business meetings. Her hesitation to mingle with people, which was the outcome of pain and loss, gave way to clarity to a large extent! Though she had not overcome the forlorn feelings of loneliness yet, her nervousness gave way to belief and her low feelings were replaced with hope! This was a whole new world that taught her to stay alive, to survive, and she had started to love it!

#

Vicky loved money! He believed it solved most of the problems in the world. If a near one was sick, he bought the best medical facilities. He gave away large sums to child rehabilitation, alcoholic rehabilitation, old people's homes, women's shelter homes, orphanages, and he was always on the prowl to give more, as he was on the prowl to make more.

He had a strange feeling that the more he gave, the more he got. An investment banker, he made crores from the stock markets every year. He reinvested the money back for more, spent more, and made more. Now that he had taken over the construction business of his father, he wanted to build an empire. He dreamt day and night of being the man responsible for changing the skyline of Mumbai. He wanted A&A (Arora & Arora) to be the world's best construction company while Mumbai as the world's business capital.

To make this dream come true, he wanted to first buy old dying factories, clear slums and rebuild modern luxurious structures, and sell them at exorbitant prices.

He was twenty-eight, rich, and single. That made him the most eligible bachelor in town. The scion was constantly hounded, persuaded, and brainwashed by the high-society women for their daughters and young women for marriage. On his part, he wanted to take it slow and surrender to 'the one person' he believed would make him happy for the rest of his life. He wanted his life partner to have her own identity, simply because he did not want a trophy wife! Besides, high-society women bored him to death.

Vicky knew that to find such a woman was difficult, but he was ready to wait.

The transformation into a practical, decision-making, quick-thinking professional businessman was not easy. It was a gradual painful process of transformation from boyhood to man. At school, Vicky was quiet, dreamy, and susceptible to people.

Till he came in the ninth grade . . . suddenly one day, his silence changed to drumbeats because of Miss Sonali, who came to teach them botany and biology—the subjects he hated the most. Sonali Teacher was young, slim, and fair, with rosy lips, large watery eyes, and a youthful bosom that made botany and biology more interesting than ever!

Every boy in the Champion Public school (South Mumbai, where Vicky did his sr. schooling) loved Sonali Teacher. Vicky too had feelings for her. He loved watching her stealthily from his corner in the class. While she read out the text, checked their notebooks, when she was sighing, when she was agitated—all these expressions of Sonali Teacher played a huge role in Vicky's life. Her face was engraved in his memory. Sonali ma'am's youthful figure, face, and her talks influenced Vicky's budding manhood. He wanted to protect her, save her, rescue her. Sometimes, he even made love to her in James Bond style (in his daydreams) while she was taking their class!

Vicky took special interest in botany and biology that year and learnt his lessons much in advance for her classes! He started scoring highest in class tests. He was so madly besotted by Sonali Teacher that he saw her in everything he did. He learnt something else too, along botany and biology—'To surrender unconditionally to the one he loved!'

"Wow, great!" she would say. "Lovely answer, you are bright, Vicky!" He would blush a beetroot red!

"Keep it up" or "Now collect the notebooks, Vicky. Please?" she would say sweetly. She rewarded him with that lopsided smile and a sigh at the end of his collection, which meant everything to him. That meant a heave from that youthful bosom too, which he so much adored, made love to in his daydreams, and wanted to shade it from the world. While taking rounds in the class, Sonali Teacher sometimes came up from behind and patted him on the back. He loved the touch. He just wanted her to pat him, standing there all day. Life was beautiful and Sonali ma'am made it so. This went on for a month, till one day he went to the lab for experiments.

A cockroach was lying pinned on a dissection board . . . Vicky hated insects but he loved Sonali Teacher, so he concentrated . . . Sonali Teacher was explaining the accuracy of the cuts. She said, "The precision with which you measure to cut is critical." Sonali went painstakingly to each child to explain the experiment. She came to Vicky's table too, to hold his hand, to help him dissect.

All the while, he was waiting for her to come to his table with bated breath. His reverie was shattered when she did. Sonali Teacher's hand was on his as he had envisioned, but she had two conjoined thumbs. In a moment, Vicky's vision of a perfect beauty fell apart! His world fell apart! He was haunted by her hand instead of her youthful body. The hand came everywhere—in her smiles, pats, heaving youthful bosom, figure! Everywhere! Now he wanted to protect her more out of pity than out of love. Vicky did not know that only the raging hormones of adolescence were playing havoc with his emotions!

After a few months, beautiful Sonali ma'am with 'conjoined thumbs' got married and left school. She disappeared as suddenly as she had appeared.

In the same grade, he fell in love with Suman. She was the girl of his dreams. She had long brown hair, wheatish complexion, and long, long everlasting legs. She could, with one touch of her finger, drive him crazy; he wanted to gift her the whole Galaxy . . . his day began and ended with her . . . she sent him arousing SMSs. Her picture was his screen saver on mobile and personal computer. They hung out a lot. They smooched and made half-baked love behind the school building after the basketball games in the evening shadows. Sonali Teacher was long forgotten, but the word 'surrender' remained.

One fine day Suman broke up with Vicky, just like that! She went out with one of his friends who was a player. She broke up with him too within a month. Vicky gave his shoulder to cry on. But he could never trust her again . . . He had felt miserable . . . They stayed friends through the ninth grade. Vicky met a girl later, who was Suman's friend, the very next year. They went out for a few months but broke up later.

On the rebound, he had many affairs with girls who were fun-loving, and the phase went on till he was well into college and professional school abroad. He learnt another lesson too.

'One needed time to process and heal from one relation to be truly available for another; otherwise, one uses other people as emotional punchbags.' At the end of it all, he learnt the deeper meaning of the word 'surrender'. That was 'unconditional love'.

Now Vicky was twenty-eight, single, and raring to take on the world with his dreams. In a few years, he wanted skyscrapers to dominate Mumbai skylines. He worked day and night, charting plans meticulously, towards making it a reality. At this point, **he was searching for a construction company that had the expertise of vacating the slums so that Vicky could build his dream! He had plans for a 110-storey imposing luxury hotel, an architectural wonder named Mumbai Palace Villa**. It would house at least 100,000 guests at one time.

Vicky's original plan was to build it after the *Rajwada* Holkar Palace style, which was a blend of French, Mughal, and Maratha architecture, and situated in the ancient city of Indore. The original seven-storey structure served as the gateway to the *Rajwada* kingdom in the eleventh century BC, and Vicky's luxury hotel would serve as the gateway to the 'elite travellers' of the world. He also wanted to add Central Asian and European architecture to original *Rajwada* design, going with the times. He wanted it to be like the Taj Mahal, the pyramids . . . magnificent, grand, imposing, magnanimous, and unavoidable from anywhere in the city. In short, he wanted to create something timeless!

It was a Saturday, and Vicky was in their palatial bungalow in Mumbai's Marine Drive. It was an eight-storey luxury home, overlooking the Arabian Sea. Ancient but revamped, his 'house-home' was a landmark and could pass off as a heritage building. It was so huge that he spoke to his parents either on the intercom or the mobile whenever he was around.

The elderly Mr Arora looked after the business from home, while the younger Vicky operated from the two offices in town. He was engrossed in going through a report sent by Maurya Builders (who were interested in a partnership with A&A) about clearing of the slums, which was taking long. Vicky had plans to start his project in a couple of months and thus could not afford the delay.

He called a number.

"What happened to the vacating job, Mihir?" Mihir was their ground engineer entrusted with the entire vacating process.

"The slum dwellers are not ready to budge, sir."

"What is the reason?"

"They have a leader, and he is instigating them not to."

"Oh! Hmmm?"

"With new demands . . . sir."

"New demands? Did not you guys tell them about the brand new houses we will be providing? What are their demands . . . anyway?" Vicky wanted to know.

"One, they do not want to go far to settle as their families have lived generation after generation in the present place, working in the adjoining factories, near to the airport that serves as their bread and butter! Second, they are demanding bigger homes of at least 500 square feet rather than the 350 square feet, promised by us. Also, some more money for each family as a compensation."

"How much?"

"Five lakhs instead of two."

"Along with the houses?"

"Yes . . . sir."

"How many families in there?"

"Around 500 . . ."

"How many estimated people?"

"Around 5,000 . . . sir."

"Umm, OK!"

"Each family has, on an average, six children," Mihir said.

"Holy Mother!" Vicky swore.

"This is India, sir!" . . . Mihir pronounced, amused.

"I know, I know this is India, my country too, and I love it."

"Yes, sir!"

"I want to make it the best! I find this demand exorbitant and unreasonable, though!"

"This could be the pretext not to move out from the place!" Mihir said. "The slum dwellers have lived there for generations, and their psyche is laced with previous bad experiences of promises made by the wealthy, looking for opportunities at their expense!"

"True! Could be that. It could be just the comfort zone! Anyways, we need the land, and we need to work towards it! That's the bottom line. You said there was someone instigating them. Who is it?"

"This guy called Gaurav . . . Gaurav Naik. All the slum dwellers idolise and worship him."

"Can we meet him for one-on-one for a settlement sometime?"

"Why not, sir. I can arrange for it!"

"OK! Let me think about it! I will get back to you. Thanks."

"Thank you, sir!"

Vicky went into deep thought after hanging up.

He had to find a way of evacuating the place! His dream could not wait any longer!

Along with the other envelopes and mail, a latest edition of **AFTER TEA** was lying on the desk with the headline **Eat for That Slim Waist!** That caught Vicky's attention instantaneously! Though his mind was occupied, he could not stop picking it to file through the pages.

Within minutes he had scanned through all the pages hungrily. It was refreshing, new, trendy, and insightful to say the least. The cover page complimented the articles inside. The models were sexy, attractive, and fresh. It was an outcome of a live shoot; unlike the previous editors who used borrowed pictures, Ananya had made use of real people! That made a welcoming difference!

'An aunty or an adolescent can equally relate to this magazine! The language is so easy to follow!' Vicky nodded to himself. 'The Indian and Western outfits are just perfect and the backdrop?' He had visited this restaurant. 'It is Shatranj Napoli! The whole issue seems to be a smash hit!' thought Vicky.

A message stuck on the outside cover for him read, "2,000 copies in circulation while 5,000 more are in demand."

'The magazine has suddenly picked up when it had no clientele a few months back,' Vicky mused . . .

He forgot all about the land deal. **AFTER TEA** took his whole attention. He came to the last page—The Editor's Note . . .

'It is so simple, to the point, and the message humble,' he thought again. 'This speaks volumes about the person who compiled it!' He read the crisp note with utmost interest:

No glamorous undertones, no hogging of the limelight, Ananya's picture at the end of the note was a plain black-and-white passport-size, which was partially hidden by her imposing signature! Vicky moved towards the windows.

'Nobody can miss the spark in those eyes,' he thought. 'She looks Scholarly and calm. She is different! If the publication continues this way, we will be abreast of the competition in the market very soon!'

Thoughtfully looking out of the French windows, **AFTER TEA** in hand, he saw hundreds of slums in the distance. This was Mumbai. The Indian city of his dreams, of slums, of Bollywood, of glamour. He envisioned in a flash the huge 110-storey building inviting world travellers in the distance. He saw his dream project come to life against the Mumbai skyline.

'It happens only here. Only in India in Mumbai.' At that moment, his door opened. Ramu, their old faithful servant, peeped in.

"*Baba*, the tea is ready. *Mummyji* and *Papaji* are in the lawn. If you want I can . . ."

"*Nai. Nai*," he said. "I am going down. Inform Mom."

"*Haanji, Baba*." The servant left.

Before leaving, he glanced at the copy of **AFTER TEA** at hand again. He leafed through the attractive colourful edition, unable to believe the change in the product. Those mysterious brown eyes bore into him again on the last page!

#

Again Ananya located a huge hoarding on the Western Express Highway to her right.

"Is it, or is it not?" She had worked on it so many times that she could tell even in her dreams! She inched on the road, driving at snail's pace, losing track of speed. The vehicles behind her started to honk urgently. Some people put out their heads, shouting at her. She was past listening to anything. By now, she had driven abreast a large hoarding. With her heart in her mouth, she could read only a fraction of the headline from where she was; rest she guessed 'of course'.

Get That Slim Waist by Just Eating Right, in bold "American typewriter" glared at her. She drove past it, disheartened, not able to stop long enough to galvanise on the pleasure of finding it there because of the traffic. After a few seconds, her eyes popped out, and her heart started thumping again. She located a similar hoarding on her side of the road, at a distance. It was the biggest out of the multitude displayed over the highway. She crossed under it feeling exhilarated! She felt that the models, one perched on the table and the other with salad in hand, were looking down at her. She could literally feel the whole event unfold. Above the smiling models read the punchline.

AFTER TEA Your own lifestyle magazine. Ananya's eyes brimmed. Adrenalin started rushing faster. The thrill of the moment pumped extra something into her veins! Her grip on the driving wheel tightened. She gasped, "I want the whole world to see it!"

#

Ananya's whole world was Alia! After a few months at work, she made it a point to return home early every third day to spend time with her bundle of joy! It was also because she still breast fed Alia, though she was almost ten months old. It was a Thursday. Ananya, as usual, had returned home early. She had showered and slipped into comfortable home pyjamas when the doorbell rang!

Mrs Verma was at the door. Mr Verma was always busy working late, and Mrs Verma suffered from an 'empty-nest' syndrome as her children were abroad. She would generally come to Ananya on some pretext to spend time in the evenings. On the other hand, Ananya loved Mrs Verma's elderly presence as she reminded her of her own mom. Her neighbours were a part of Ananya's extended family along with Nilesh, Richa, and other members of her team in the office.

"Is your TV working?" Mrs Verma asked from the door.

"Yes, aunty, how are you? Please come in. Is yours not working?"

"No, it is not. It just happened suddenly. Uncle is still not returned from work, and I don't know what went wrong. Maybe one of the wires is loose, and my favourite serial *Ramayan* is going to be aired on Doordarshan in a while," she went on.

"Why don't you come in?"

"Oh yes, I will come in five minutes. Please keep the door open, dear. I have a vessel on gas, and my *dal* must be simmering. I will switch it off and come," she rejoined.

She came after five minutes; little Alia recognised her and started to gurgle excitedly.

"Please be my guest and make yourself comfortable." Ananya asked, "Will you have some coffee?"

"No, no, dear! Dinner time, *na.*"

Mrs Verma's *Ramayan* started. She was a great fan of Lord Rama. She regularly watched *Mahadev* on Colors too.

"Ooohhh, my sweety pie, come to aunty," she cajoled Alia.

Alia whimpered and purred in ecstasy and started to crawl on the floor faster. Ananya meanwhile glided into the kitchen in search of food. She loaded her plate with *raita* and *pudina paratha*.

The doorbell rang again.

"I heard the voices and could not control. I thought of joining in." Mrs Mishra was at the door.

"Is your TV working?" Mrs Verma asked again from her sofa as she saw Mrs Mishra at the door.

"Yes. Yours is not? Again?"

"I think mine has a problem," informed Mrs Verma.

"Please join us," said Ananya courteously. "Have dinner. Marri has made *pudina paratha*."

"*Nai, nai*, don't bother. I have made nice *pulav*."

"It is high time we got together. I am always busy. How are you, Mrs Mishra? Are your children home?" asked Ananya.

"Yes. As you know, they are always home from college in the afternoon only, but Rajeev went to the tennis class and has not returned still. Waiting for him. He is not taking my calls also." That was a perennial complaint of Mrs Mishra that her children did not respond to her calls.

"Where does he go for the classes?"

"To the next society. They have a good instructor."

"Come in, don't stand near the door, come in," shouted Mrs Verma from the sofa.

"No, no, my Rajeev must be on way. We are preparing to sit for dinner." Turning to Ananya, she added, "Besides, you are a busy professional, a big editor. My Preeti is such a big fan of yours." Preeti was Mrs Mishra's teenaged daughter; she aspired to become a model and worked day and night in the gym for a great model's figure.

"Don't they teach tennis here in our society?" asked Ananya to Mrs Mishra.

"Ours is for renovation, don't you know, dear?"

"Is it? I am in my own world! Please come in and sit down. Sit down, *na*."Ananya requested sweetly.

"Koochi, koochi, soooo sweet . . . mama's girl, where is mama? Every day working? Recognise aunty?" Mrs Mishra cajoled Alia in baby language from the door. Alia squatted on the carpet in excitement and made happy gurgling noises.

Mrs Mishra went to her house and stood at the door, looking out at the lift eagerly, waiting for it to open. "This boy, *na,* it is already nine o'clock, never picks my calls," she mumbled worriedly.

Ananya followed her to stand at her own door, while Alia played in the background and Marriamma and Mrs Verma watched *Ramayan*.

Preeti peeked out from under her mom's hand.

"What is for dinner? *Pulav*?" she said. "I will put on weight, will have to work out vigorously."

"You and your workout!" Mrs Mishra, rejoined frustrated.

"This is the third time in the week that you made pulav, Ma!"

Mrs Mishra hated cooking. She cut the dinner short by making *pulav* or *parathas* most of the time.

"OK, OK, now set the table. Go, go," she said and nudged Preeti. Preeti made a face and retreated into the house to set the table for dinner. Ananya just laughed.

"Check the curd in the fridge and keep it as well along with the pickle," Mrs Mishra shouted over her shoulder.

Having said that, she animatedly started to gossip about the neighbourhood, standing at the door. Preeti came out in a while to say that there was very little curd, sufficient only for one.

"OK, OK!" Mrs Mishra looked a little embarrassed as if the quantity of the curd made her a bad housewife.

"Mrs Mishra, take some *raita* from my kitchen," Ananya offered. "Marri has made a lot of it."

"No, no . . . what is the need? There is pickle."

"I know, but take some. I am alone here and won't be eating all of it."

"But it is not necessary. There is pickle. We will manage."

"Please! I will not be eating all of it." Ananya insisted.

"Thank you, but it was not necessary." Ananya did not force her neighbour much after that. At that moment, Rajeev walked out of the lift.

"Hi, aunties!" He was dripping in perspiration.

"Hi, Rajeev!" said Ananya . . . 'He looks very tired, with dark circles around his eyes. He looks sick and different. Must be the studies,' Ananya thought, shrugging.

"Playing a lot of tennis?" she asked aloud.

"Yes!" he said to Ananya with a lazy, tired look.

Ananya asked again, "Rajeev! Are you OK, dear?"

"Yes!" he answered, immediately defensive.

'He looks different,' she thought. 'He is not his usual cheerful self!' She felt queer that a tired teenager had responded so sharply to her simple question, or it could be that she was over-reading him. She was very close to Mrs Mishra and, for that matter, Mrs Verma as these spirited housewives had a big hand in making her sociable again! She, in turn, felt overprotective about them and their families!

After chatting for a couple of minutes, Mrs Mishra excused herself, and Ananya retreated into her home. Mrs Verma was watching her favourite serial *Ramayan* on Doordarshan with reverence, along with Marriamma. Every time Lord Ram or Sita came on the screen, she joined her hands in a namaste. Ananya smiled to herself in amusement.

"Mrs Verma, have dinner with me," she requested again.

"No, no! Not until the serial is over. I have cooked *baigan ka bharta, na*. Mr Verma's favourite. We will have dinner at home."

Ananya was famished and slurped at the *raita* and *parathas*, sitting on the carpet itself, while Alia played around happily.

"It's a boon for me to have neighbours like you. I can come to watch these, these serials! I can always fall back on you whenever I want," said Mrs Verma unnecessarily in the commercial break.

"It's the other way round actually. It is you and Mrs Mishra who look after Alia in my absence. You are family. You run innumerable outside errands too. Who will do so much?"

Mrs Verma looked impressed at Ananya's rejoinder and swung her head happily! "When will your mom come home, dear?" she asked before concentrating back on the serial.

"She will."

"I don't know when these people are going to show the real *swayamvar*. They are showing the Ram and Sita romance since the past four episodes," Mrs Verma complained in the next break. That day too the episode ended without the *swayamvar*.

Mrs Verma hung on, chatting with Ananya for some time before going home that night.

Ananya sat in front of the television for some time after her neighbour left, watching TLC's *Bizzare* show by Andrew Zimmerns. He was popping live crabs into his mouth after breaking the tentacles. It was disgusting.

Ananya skipped channels. A programme about a drug called methamphetamine was on Discovery channel.

'Who took them?' she thought before yawning deeply.

She switched to a news channel that was airing the story of some scams in the city—how the rich builders were ditching the poor slum dwellers in the name of providing free homes.

Ananya wondered if she could do a story on scams for **AFTER TEA.**

'I am too tired now to think about it.' She plonked next to her already sleeping baby on the bed and pulled the neat sheets over both of them. That night, Rajeev's face played in her memory before she fell into deep sleep.

She had just walked out of the conference room at three in the afternoon, when her mobile rang. It was Marriamma. Generally, she never called at this hour. It so happened that Ananya had to rush immediately from office to a government hospital in Borivali. Rajeev was admitted because of a drug overdose!

She could not believe that her stray observation that 'the youngster was not himself' had come true!

"Nobody knew about it in the family, . . ." whispered Mrs Verma. Mrs Mishra found him unconscious in his room after he returned from college. "They will shift him to a rehab after he comes to his senses. This is a police case; so they brought him to a government hospital." **Rajeev's inert body inserted with syringes lay on the bed as they spoke.**

"Oh God . . ." Ananya gasped, looking at him.

Mrs Mishra came out crying. Ananya, along with Mrs Verma, followed her into the doctor's cabin. A police officer was already present in the room.

"He will be all right! Don't worry. You will see. He is going to overcome this phase quickly," Ananya consoled Mrs Mishra without conviction.

In low doses, **methamphetamine** increases alertness, but in high doses, anything can happen from euphoria, psychosis, or even death. It is a prescription II drug abroad.

'Oh!' Ananya remembered watching a programme on it. She went numb with goosebumps!

"My child was having drugs under my nose? Oh God!" wept Mrs Mishra as her husband held her for support.

"We will know why he was taking such a drug when he comes to his senses," the police officer added. Mrs Mishra wailed more.

A slow anger mixed with turmoil started to rise inside Ananya. She could not fathom the pain these simple neighbours of hers must be experiencing! Who were these people on the prowl? How could they, in the first place, manage to sell poison to youngsters? Where did this all happen in the city? How many youngsters were slaves to drugs in the very neighbourhood she lived? How many parents were getting manipulated in handing out that extra buck for buying drugs by their own children? Could she or anyone bring the drug pedlars to book? Could she do anything at all?

Unable to bear the consuming pain in the room, she followed the doctor out. "Hi, I am Ananya. I am a neighbour and a friend of the couple. Will Rajeev get well?" she asked the doctor, introducing herself.

"We have him under observation. We will see." The doc introduced himself. "I am Dr Dixit, a paediatric, specialised in skin ailments."

Ananya looked at him quizzically. "Skin ailments?"

"The docs here were clueless as there were blisters all over the boy's body. So they contacted me. A rash is an external manifestation of a major internal illness or a drug . . ." his voice trailed. "I came here for my usual round of social work and landed on the case."

Ananya was impressed. "I am a journalist."

"Oh!"

"If I am doing a story on drug addiction, I will definitely contact you."

"Sure!" The doc handed her his card with the number.

She did not know that she would call him very soon.

#

While returning from a meeting in Pune's Le Meridian (the previous day), Vicky shifted restlessly in his seat. He wanted fast work. His dream project in Mumbai was going nowhere. It was Tuesday. He planned to close the deals by the weekend. He checked his watch; it was nine o'clock. He dialled his secretary Stella's number.

"Stella?" She had just reached office.

"Yes, sir?"

"Can you please quickly run me through today's schedule?"

"Sir, please give me five minutes?"

"OK!"

Vicky's phone rang exactly in five minutes.

"Sir?"

"Yes?"

"You have a meeting with the board for the upcoming project 'Mumbai Palace Villa'. A few designers from Dubai will also be present, at eleven o'clock."

"Oh! I remember now. Did you?"

Stella responded immediately, "They have been put up in Grand Maratha. I have arranged for their transport to the office and back, sir."

"Good."

"Lunch with the same group, sir, at 1.30 p.m. in the office itself. Then a meeting at three with Mr Gaurav, the union leader, . . . from Bhairavi Slums."

"OK?"

Vicky thought quickly.

"Please cancel the meeting with this union leader . . . Besides, after the board meeting, I won't be in a proper frame of mind to converse with this fellow."

"I understand, sir. I will call him to cancel the meeting."

"That's all?"

"All the meetings are at the Oshiwara office, sir."

"I will call you if anything comes up. Thanks!"

"Have a great day, sir!" The phone went dead.

Vicky settled back on his cushiony seat. This SUV he used for travelling was a four-wheeled luxury. It had foam cushions, adjustable seats on either side of the vehicle like a limousine, a small enclosed space for the driver, a television set, with latest audio technology, top-of-the-line air conditioning and climate control systems, tinted windows for privacy, finest upholstery and interiors, and a standard counter built-in refrigerator, stacked with drinks from around the world.

Vicky had started for Mumbai without his morning brew. He checked the inbuilt fridge. His eyes moved over mojito, cider, shikuwasa juice, fanta, and raksi, which sent a burning sensation down the throat but melted effortlessly, once inside. He was tempted to have raksi, his favourite, but he opened a can of tomato juice instead. He could almost hear his mom complain.

"Don't drink cold juices early morning, Vicky." He smiled and took a gulp of the chilled juice. He looked out of the speeding vehicle. Beautiful pink, red, and white bougainvillea adorned the expressway!

His mind was racing.

Vicky was restless to grow his empire in and around Mumbai. He wanted to create a sensation. He had seen his father work round the clock with large building designs, taking board meetings, and making plans over the phone. Vicky wanted to make history, wanted his company's name on the world map. Twenty-four hours in a day were not enough!

He opened his mail. He started to speedily go through the mails sent by Stella. He opened the mail on Gaurav the union leader, who was the obstruction in starting their dream project.

Vicky read: Gaurav was twenty-seven, a graduate, and jobless; he took up small jobs from the surrounding industries to burn his home fire. God-fearing, teetotaller, and a great devotee of lord Ganesha. He fasted on all the eleven days of the year during the *Ganesha* festival. He personally worshipped the Elephant God during the festivities in Bhairavi Slums. He inspired poor slum dwellers by his fiery speeches. They, in turn, looked up to him as a young inspiring leader. He lived with his mother, a widow; his father was a farmer.

Gaurav was constantly instigating the slum dwellers not to budge.

Vicky could not think of building his dream anywhere in the city. The area where Bhairavi Slums stood was near to the international airport next to the ocean. It was exclusive and accessible to international travellers!

"Stella? How did you get Gaurav's info?"

"From Mr Braganza, our private detective, sir!"

"Can you SMS me Mr Braganza's number?"

"Sure, sir!" She did.

Vicky dialled Mr Braganza.

He took the call at the seventh ring.

"Mr Braganza?"

"Yes?"

"I am Vicky Arora from Arora & Arora."

"Of course! Of course! Tell me, sir, how may I help you?" Mr Braganza spoke in a slight accent!

"I was going through the details sent by you about Gaurav from Bhairavi Slums. I was wondering if you could feed me more personal information on this guy?"

"From Bhairavi Slums? Ummm, let me see. I think we got more information about him. Please give me five minutes."

"Sure!" The phone went dead.

Mr Braganza called after ten minutes.

"He has some ancestral land in a small village called Rampur," the detective said. "I thought of not giving this information as it was not concerning the slums."

"OK! Give me every detail about this fellow now."

"He has been fighting a battle for almost two decades now for the land with no results."

"OK?"

"It is just a two-acre ancestral land he is fighting for with the local *sarpanch*."

"OK?"

"The *sarpanch* took away their land," Braganza continued. "It was some twenty years back, with the promise to return it once the money was paid of course! Gaurav's family could not return the paltry sum. Gaurav's father died under mysterious circumstances."

"Mysterious circumstances?"

"He was found hanging from the *peepal* tree that grew on their land."

"Villagers say it was a suicide, but Gaurav's mom believes that it was a murder. Planned by the evil *sarpanch*. The mother came to Mumbai soon after and worked as a domestic help to bring up her son."

"Now her son is fighting a bitter battle against the *sarpanch* for the land and to avenge the death of his father?" Vicky observed, "What a Hindi film story!"

"Yes, sir," Braganza laughed.

Suddenly Vicky was excited.

"Mr Braganza, can you find out the details of Gaurav's case? I want anything and everything you guys can lay hands on."

"Sir!" Mr Braganza said, "Give me a couple of days, and I will mail you the details with the photographs."

"Sure! That will be great! Thank you. You have a great day, Mr Braganza!" said Vicky and hung up.

Vicky read other mails.

Sri Agastya of Platinum Nest Builders was in his mid-thirties. He was into real estate for the past five years now. Vicky went through his personal details quickly for the upcoming dream project.

Educated from Mumbai's Sydenham college, married to his high school girlfriend, he did roaring business of buying and selling property and stocks; he had a son who was in the seventh standard. He was a small-time businessman a few years back.

His USP? Evacuating slums within hours. He was aspiring to stand for the local elections too. Mr Agastya wanted to go into a 25 per cent partnership with A&A to build 'Mumbai Palace Villa'.

Vicky leant back in his seat; his mind was racing again . . .

'I can use this guy to evacuate the slums. If he is good at it, I will give him the 25 per cent partnership for that matter to whoever impresses me,' he thought.

He checked his watch. It was 10.30 and he was famished. In a while, his SUV neared the outskirts of Panvel. He leant forward to instruct his driver.

Within half an hour, they were outside Swad restaurant, a small veg eatery that dished out the best *pav bhaji* and *masala* dosas.

Vicky had a lot of mails to check, so he did not get out for breakfast; instead, he asked Mahesh, "Get me a *rava masala*," his favourite.

In a while, his burly driver handed him *rava masala* dosa and piping hot coffee in a plastic cup. The dosas were crisp, hot, and the *masala* inside was of the right taste; the coffee was creamy, sweet, hot, and delicious.

It was the month of March; the day was catching on, but there was still a slight chill in the breeze. Vicky cherished the dosa in his vehicle. The birds chirped on the trees, and the small restaurant was quiet in the morning sun; such experiences were priceless for him.

Mahesh dutifully came back in fifteen minutes after his breakfast and manoeuvred the vehicle on to the highway expertly. Vicky could see his favourite city come into focus.

"Oshiwara office," he directed his driver.

#

Ananya was not going to her usual Oshiwara office that Tuesday. She was going to Igatpuri with Richa in their office vehicle.

Ananya was doing a story on 'alternative healing'. She was travelling to a Buddhist meditation centre in Igatpuri, and later on in the day, she was to visit Urvashi Manpekar, an NLP exponent in Goregaon.

"Hope we have a good experience," said Ananya.

"Yes, ma'am! I am a little nervous, though," rejoined Richa.

"You know, Urvashi was an actress in her heydays?"

"Oh! I know, ma'am. She was a very successful actress, also very beautiful. She must be forty-plus?"

"Around . . . forty-five!"

"Am eager to meet her," said Richa.

"Me too."

"What is NLP?"

"It is the neurolinguistic programming of the brain, I guess. That is what I read."

"Neurolinguistic?" Richa repeated after Ananya "Of the brain? I have heard 'linguistic'. I never heard of a brain language. Strange," Richa laughed.

"I wanted to compare these two modalities of healing and present them as relevant to modern living."

They were working on a story on alternative healing techniques that could burst stress in the cities like Mumbai! Ananya chose 'stress' as a topic for their upcoming issue as it was the most plaguing modern lifestyle hurdle. The two modalities Ananya wanted to write were 'ancient' and 'modern'. She decided to merge them to come up with a solution for present-day existence. She looked fondly at Richa.

She was reading *The Style Diary of a Bollywood Diva* by Kareena Kapoor with Rachelle Pinto. She had the latest edition of *Vogue* as well with Kareena on the cover.

"You are a great fan of Kareena Kapoor! Ain't you?"

"Yes, ma'am! She has an easy style I love."

Ananya smiled.

"I am going to write a book one day," Richa said. "About all my experiences."

"All the best! I think journalists do that after their heydays are over, like actresses are into NLP or yoga." Both laughed heartily. "Now we must reach fast. The Buddhist monk will be waiting for us," added Ananya. Both giggled like children.

Richa went back to reading her book while Ananya was lost in Alia's thoughts. She was fast asleep at six when she had left home. She was teething and fell sick often. Ananya constantly worried about her. She was planning to wind up the day early, after the interviews, and go home.

The vehicle caught up speed towards their destination.

#

The vipassana meditation centre in Igatpuri was encased in greenery and was situated on top of a small hillock. As they approached the ashram-temple, they saw huge carved pillars, with a dome. The entrance looked like a pagoda. The whole place was like a landscape out of a painting. Bhikkuji *Maharaj*, the saint in charge of the ashram, was waiting for them; he had a shaven head and wore long flowing orange robes. He looked every inch a Buddhist monk.

He greeted them with folded hands.

Richa and Ananya exchanged glances before bowing to the saint.

'He must be in his early thirties!' Ananya guessed.

"This way please!" They were comfortably seated in his temple office in a few minutes.

"I am Ananya, and she is Richa, my colleague. I spoke to you about the meditation and the interview yesterday?"

"Yes, yes," said the saint gently.

Ananya asked at length, "How is it that meditation can cure diseases and stress?"

"By bringing peace and happiness to the mind!"

"Oh!" Richa reacted sharply. Ananya smiled at her.

"On a more spiritual level, we can find various principles and practices which can be used to bring peace and happiness to the mind and good health to the body," said the saint.

Ananya could hear a group praying in the background.

"We would love to see the ashram," said she.

"Come with me."

Bhikkuji walked them through the courtyard. There was a beautiful fountain of clear water with a five-petal lotus at the centre. The petals were large and pink, and the sound of gurgling water was soothing. The morning birds twittered above in the trees as a squirrel went up the tree trunk with a nut. The place had a surreal peace to it.

Bhikkuji sat down on the small wall surrounding the fountain and signalled them to do the same.

Both sat.

"The chanting is a way of going into deep meditation. It also wards off evil spirits." Richa looked alarmed, and Ananya wanted to laugh.

"A group of saints", Bhikkuji said, "practise here the ancient methods of treatment proposed by the Buddhist monks. An emphasis on understanding how nature works in our lives. Actually, living a holistic life doesn't only mean eating a natural diet. It also means changing and correcting our lifestyle by learning how to meditate, learning how to reduce stress in everyday life." They both nodded like children.

"But coming to the point, how does meditation cure?" Richa persisted.

"Come with me." He walked them to a large hall where hundreds of devotees were chanting in unison.

"They are doing a fifteen-day course in vipassana meditation," the saint informed them.

He quietly signalled them to follow him. Ananya and Richa stood at the back door while the group of saints chanted their morning prayers with the devotees.

Bhikkuji *Maharaj* stood there for some time and asked them to follow him into the meditation hall. By now, the chanting had stopped and the crowd was quiet. They all entered from the back doors and sat silently. Bhikkuji signalled them to close their eyes as a saint instructed the healing meditation on a mike in English.

"Take a few deep breaths and relax. Let the thoughts flow. Do not obstruct any thought coming to your mind . . . relax . . . relax . . . relax. Allow the stress to flow out of your body. Now take your attention to that part of the body or an organ that is ailing."

'Ailing?' Ananya remembered her toe was aching for some time now because of her many adventures around Alia. She took her attention there.

"Now concentrate totally on the ailing organ or the part. Visualise the universal healing white light passing through your body to all the parts from your crown chakra. See the light go to every part, every nook and corner of your body, including the ailing organ. Feel the light cleanse the organ, as if you are doing a mental surgery to it. Visualise the pain, the ailment, evaporate from it. Do it several times . . . do it very slowly . . . feeling it . . . feeling the pain evaporate . . . Now visualise the organ as 'whole and healthy' without any disease . . . feel and know that it is healed. Believe that it is healed . . . feel the compassionate love of the light . . . thank the white light for healing the organ . . ."

It went on for a long time. The saint was repeating the same instructions again and again like a mantra. Then there was silence.

Ananya fell asleep.

After some time, she could hear some instructions as if from a distance. "Open your eyes. Please open your eyes, slowly please."

Ananya forced open her eyes. She moved her toe vigorously; the pain was less! She moved it and again the pain was less. 'How could her simple concentration cure an aching toe?' She was impressed. She could not wait to put it on paper. Share it with her readers.

It was 11.30 by the time it ended.

"Buddhist saints have only two meals per day," Bhikkuji informed them as he took them to their beautiful neat ashram canteen for lunch later.

Ananya nodded, blinking. They had some lentils, boiled vegetables, and soya extracts with rice.

"I will send you a copy of the magazine," she said while leaving and bowed for blessings. The saint nodded. He looked very neutral as though he could do without the worldly publicity.

They left Igatpuri.

Richa gave the Goregaon address to their driver for their next session. "*Teli galli*, bungalow number 7, near Hanuman *Mandir*, Goregaon—West." Urvashi took NLP sessions in her small bungalow there. Her secretary greeted them and ushered them into the office immediately.

Urvashi was nothing like a modern-age guru. She looked every inch a diva. She was glamourously dressed in a long gown and smiled at them.

"Welcome! Press is always late, especially now that I am no more in the movies," she joked.

"We are sorry! But the traffic was bad. We are coming from Igatpuri."

"Oh! I see? Please be seated." A maid brought water for them.

"Tea, coffee?" asked Urvashi.

"No, no! Please let's get on with the interview. We are already late," said Ananya.

Urvashi came to the point straight . . . "Hope you have heard about NLP?"

"Yes, I did a bit of reading," informed Ananya.

"NLP is all about reprogramming your mind. We all know that we have subconscious mind that works in spite of us. The unwanted things that happen to us are the experiences we have invited into our lives unknowingly through the subconscious."

It was very exciting for Richa . . . "Wow! Wish fulfilment! Lovely!" she exclaimed.

Ananya suppressed a smile.

"Kind of!" said Urvashi.

"I want to know how and why you came into NLP since you were such a famous celebrity," asked Ananya.

"I just bumped into my teacher Nilkanth, who was an exponent of NLP, and I was so impressed by it that I wanted to dedicate my life to this amazing technique."

"Wow!" exclaimed Richa.

"Great!" added Ananya.

"You can change your life by just going deeper and deeper into your subconscious. NLP works on the principles of manifestation through visualisation. I will put you into a trance and guide you through the process of neurolinguistic programming (NLP). It is one of the time-tested tools to achieve financial, relationship, or career success. It can take you to the highest possible standards determined by you and you alone!"

"What is the process of going into a trance?" Richa asked nervously.

"I will show you a swinging crystal. You have to concentrate on it. I will count up to ten and ask you some questions. Then count backwards and test if you are ready. Then you will lie down, and I will guide you through the process. It's very simple."

"As it is a general session, I will take both of you in. Otherwise, I take only one client at a time."

Urvashi stood up. She asked them to follow her; they entered a small room with dim lights. Two neat beds with white bed covers were on either side of the room. A small side table was in a corner with a wooden focus light. A strong waft of fragrance hit them as they entered. The table was decorated with lighted aromatic candles and incense sticks and rose petals. Otherwise, the room was enclosed and simple.

"Wow! What a setting," Richa whispered . . . Nervousness palpable in her voice! "I know what to ask—my ex." She giggled. "Or for some food, the lentils have already digested."

"Shhhhhh, no jokes . . . hope everything goes well." There was a shiver in Ananya's voice. She glanced at the watch on the wall. It was exactly two in the afternoon.

Ananya went into trance quickly. Richa took some time. Both of them were sleeping on the beds in ten minutes. Urvashi started her guidance.

"Totally relax your minds, and at the count of ten you will start visualising."

"Relax, totally relax . . . take a few deep breaths . . . now, 1 . . . 2 . . . 3 . . . 4 . . . 5 . . . 6 . . . 10, start visualising . . . what do you want in life the most? What do you aspire to be? Do you want to be rich? Then visualise all the wealth in the world . . . visualise everything that money can buy . . . a private plane, yacht, 100 homes . . . billions of dollars—anything and everything. Accounts running in crores in a Swiss bank. If you cannot, then visualise a Aladdin's cave . . . with all the wealth in it, and add more to it on your own," Urvashi joked.

'Is joking allowed during NLP?' Ananya thought.

"Do you want the best body? Healthy body? Go all for it. See yourself having a smoky sexy body! The best figure in the world. You want success? Do you want name and fame? Visualise it because it shall be yours."

Ananya was really feeling funny at this point! She had some doubt 'How was it pos . . . ?'

"Do not doubt anything," Urvashi said, and Ananya jumped out of her doubtful thoughts.

"Visualise people asking for your autographs. Pining for you, loving you more than anything in the world . . . Believe that it is all yours . . . that shall happen."

Funny . . . In the trance, Ananya did not feel any different. She just felt as if she was lying down and listening to someone. She could hear all the instructions clearly. She went about visualising a happy family. In the happy family Alia was there, Marriamma was there, her mom was there, and she herself was there. She played with the baby, enjoyed a warm family time in a cosy home. She saw herself as a great mom.

"Go all about it! Visualise."

On remembering to write about a solution by merging the two modalities, Ananya decided to experiment. She brought in the light from the Buddhist meditation that morning. With that light, she cleansed her home, thanked her baby . . . her little world, all the people in there for making it wonderful . . . her neighbours . . . friends . . . colleagues . . . she blessed Rahul for being there as a parent, a partner, a great lover . . . cleansed herself, home, child . . . now?

'Is crying allowed?'

"Go all about it, ask what you want." The instructions went on.

Next she saw enough of wealth for herself and her baby . . . a fleet of cars . . . a penthouse. She saw herself writing the best stories. She saw people appreciating those stories. 'Now?'

"Go all about it!"

"Lots of bank balance."

"Visualise!"

Ananya saw . . . saw . . . saw . . . walking the red carpet . . . 'But why not? Who knows what I am thinking?' She laughed to herself.

"Don't doubt it, see it, feel it . . . visualise and know . . . it's going to happen!"

'I am walking the red carpet . . . let's see . . . in a white satin gown . . . no . . . black, no red . . . yes red, red flowing satin gown . . . the one like Ange wore for Globe Awards . . . red flowing satin gown . . . with slight frills at the bustier.'

"Don't stop, visualise! What do you see now . . . ? Just concentrate on it. Go all about it all about it . . . don't hesitate . . ." Urvashi went on instructing.

'I am walking in a red flowing satin gown with frills. At the bustier and . . . ?'

"Give clear instructions to your mind."

'Red flowing satin gown . . . with lace all over, no . . . light lacy frills hugging my bosom. A little exposure at the . . . breast . . . will look good, ya . . . ya, I love those gowns . . . that expose at the same time leave a lot to the imagination!'

"Visualise! Don't stop."

'My hair is up with sparkling little diamond pins, a strand falling over my forehead. Two small diamond studs . . . SEXY! A big rock on my left-hand ring finger . . . to compliment the earrings . . . LOVELY!'

"Go all about it . . ."

'I am walking to an awards function. Wow! What nonsense! Is it really going to . . . ?'

"Go all about it . . . make it very clear . . . instruct your mind . . ."

'I am walking to . . . to this awards function, in a palace by the sea . . .'

"Feel it, feel it . . . don't doubt it . . ."

'I am going to this awards function in a palace? God! The crowd . . . it's reckless. It's crazy . . . the press . . . the media . . . people are calling . . . calling my name . . . interviews . . . TV channels . . . every channel . . . '

"Feel it, feel it . . ."

Ananya put all the feelings of euphoria, of elation . . . she fell into a deep slumber . . . at this point.

"Know that it is going to happen . . ." Urvashi was saying. "Never for a second doubt it! Your mind is the most powerful tool . . ."

When she came to, she was alone in the room. Ananya slowly got up; she felt a little groggy but totally relaxed. She was full of energy, as if she had just woken in the morning. She had a strange sense of fulfilment as well.

She walked out into the office . . . Urvashi asked her gently, "Want to drink water?" and passed on a glass of crystal clear water in her direction.

"How do you feel?"

"Great!" said Ananya.

"You fell asleep. It happens most of the times as the mind concentrates hard . . . don't worry, whatever you have visualised has gone to the subconscious."

Ananya looked at the clock on the wall; it was 3.30 in the afternoon. She had slept for a full one and half hours.

After profuse 'thank yous', they left.

Richa wanted to take a cab from the highway. Ananya and Richa sat in the vehicle. Ananya directed the driver towards her home and fished for her mobile and switched it on.

"Thirty-seven missed calls? Who the hell? Marriamma?" Ananya panicked.

"What happened, ma'am?" asked Richa, alarmed too.

Ananya called home. Instead of Marriamma, Mrs Verma took the call. She blurted out incoherently, "Ananya! Ananya! Alia is having high temperature, not drinking or eating anything . . . her face and neck are swollen."

"Oh my God!" Ananya's heart was in her mouth. "I am on my way. Is she active?" She asked in a shaking voice.

"No, she is sleeping, with high temperature! Marriamma was trying to reach out to you but could not! Please come home immediately."

"Oh God! Oh my God . . . Oh my God!" Ananya was in tears.

"What happened, ma'am?" asked the driver too, looking over his shoulder anxiously.

"Oh God, my baby . . . it seems she is very sick, having high temperature . . . Oh God . . . I don't know . . . she is very sick." Ananya started shivering.

"Oh God! Ma'am . . . may I help you in some way?"

Ananya was past listening to anyone . . . little Alia's face was playing in front of her eyes now.

The highway came fast . . .

Richa got down uncertainly. "Please let me know if you want anything. Call me, ma'am." She lingered at the door.

Ananya could just nod.

#

Richa stood on the Western Express Highway for some time after Ananya left! She was shaken with the sudden developments in the day! She wanted to speak to someone! She dialled Nilesh. He took the call almost immediately.

"Ananya ma'am, Ananya ma'am!"

"Ananya ma'am? What happened to her?"

"Ananya ma'am's baby is serious. She is very, very serious . . . Yes, yes, we have finished the interviews, but she is in a bad shape. She has gone home . . . the baby seems to be serious," Richa blurted out all at once.

Manish and Alok (another technical support) were hovering around Nilesh at that time.

"Ananya ma'am's baby is serious," Nilesh informed them.

Manish and Alok went to their cubicles, discussing the news.

"Sick? My God! Something serious must have happened. She says ma'am was crying."

Raghav, the peon, came around.

"Who was crying?"

"Ananya ma'am," informed Alok. "Her baby is serious."

"Oh God!" Raghav went out . . . He met a couple of accountants and engineers from the construction department . . . near the water cooler . . .

"Ananya ma'am's baby is not well. She is in a critical condition. She is admitted in the hospital. In the ICU," he added on his own.

"Critical? Who is admitted?

"Who is Ananya?" asked another.

The news spread like wildfire in the office.

Ananya held her baby very close. Alia's eyes were closed, and her body was burning hot. Her face was swollen, and the breathing was strained. She soiled her diapers too often. Ananya brought her to a super-speciality hospital nearby, accompanied by Mrs Verma.

'God, don't let anything happen to my baby please,' Ananya prayed, as Alia's body felt warmer by the hour!

The Neonatal Care unit of Sanjeevani Hospital was separate from other sections; the children's ward was huge with fifty-nine rooms. It had an observation unit, high dependency unit . . . HDU, all American style.

Ananya was past looking at anything. She was only conscious of the bundle in her hands. Now Alia was getting irritable and started to whimper. Mrs Verma was not allowed inside the examination room, so she waited outside.

Five doctors were attending to Alia in the leadership of Dr Malhotra, a middle-aged paediatric surgeon and specialist.

Ananya stood in a corner silently, observing them.

A doctor checked Alias's heartbeat while another checked her entire body. Dr Malhotra took her temperature, a lady doctor gingerly pressed her stomach, an ENT surgeon examined her too, and a nurse stood with a tray with some instruments. The Emergency Ward reverberated with Alia's cries.

"It's 103 degrees." Dr Malhotra moved his head. "It's very high for a small baby . . . I can see a slight swelling in the throat." . . . He touched Alias's throat gingerly, and she started to cry more loudly.

The doctors exchanged glances.

"Running nose," observed another.

"I can see some rash on the torso and legs," said Dr Lata, the lady doctor in attendance "It's very unusual . . . hope . . ." Her voice trailed, and Ananya worried more!

'Oh God, what is it . . . what has happened to my baby? Please, God.' Ananya stood there, praying.

"Once the symptoms are located, we can prescribe a treatment, otherwise . . . difficult."

Dr Malhotra signalled to the nurse.

"Prepare for a sponge bath to bring down the temperature."

He turned to his team. "First, let us work on bringing down the temperature. Once it's down, we will keep the baby for observation before taking a call. Temperature and rash, bad combination," he blurted out.

The observation went on for an hour with no results. After the sponging, the temperature came down by a degree, but the doctors could not exactly pinpoint Alias's ailment.

Ananya stood there observing the doctors helplessly. It was almost an hour. Her baby looked worse than before. Her rash seemed to have increased on the neck. Her nose was constantly watering. She was more listless, but the doctors could not come to a diagnosis. By now Ananya lost her patience and was fuming from within. "She needs rest and food!" Ananya almost wailed at the team of doctors suddenly!

"We are trying our best, Mrs Bhatt," said Dr Malhotra. "I know how you feel."

"You are doctors. You should know the ailment . . . but . . . but you don't seem to?"

"We need a paediatric skin specialist, I think . . . as our specialist is out of town . . . we are trying . . . for some other doctor. Please keep patience, Mrs Bhatt," said Dr Malhotra, his voice rising in frustration.

Ananya started to sob softly. All the doctors stared at her helplessly!

"What does a skin specialist got to do with fever?" Ananya asked at last, once she could find her voice. 'Is she a guinea pig for experimentation?' she thought.

"Until we take a specialist's opinion, we cannot move further. Skin rash is serious!" Dr Malhotra said, exasperated.

"Skin rash is an external manifestation of a serious internal illness!" Somebody had said this to her. Ananya ran out.

"Give me my bag, Mrs Verma."

"What is it, dear? What does the doctor say?"

She frantically scrolled down all the numbers of doctors she had saved on her mobile. She could not find it, all the numbers starting with a D, she could not find it. She had not saved it.

'Fool, fool, fool,' she cried to herself.

'What am I going to do now? The only other hope is to call Mrs Mishra. He said he did social work. Could the hospital have his number, most certainly? That was the last hope. He was the one who saved Rajeev. He was the one who will save my baby, but where is he?'

"Dear, what is it? What does the doctor say?" Mrs Verma persisted nervously.

"The rash . . . they are worried . . . now who will be having Dr Dixit's number?" Ananya said more to herself . . . than to Mrs Verma.

"Dr Dixit?" Mrs Verma was clueless about such a doctor.

Ananya just dug through all the compartments of her working bag; she spilled the contents on the sofa.

Home cleaners, editors, journalists, publishers, an old card of Dr Mehta—no use—florists. The last thing she could think of now was celebration. Gift makers, boutiques, models, model coordinators, where the bloody hell was the card that she needed?

A small white card had fallen on the floor.

"Is this the one?" Mrs Verma picked the card from the floor.

Dr Dixit paediatric child specialist. SKIN.

"Dr Dixit, I got him . . . I got him," Ananya cried.

#

Dr Dixit was in the middle of an important meeting with a regular patient. His mobile was on a silent mode. It started to ring. He ignored the call. The phone started to ring persistently again. Again he ignored. Again it rang.

"Please pick up . . . please pick up . . . pick up, pick up, pick up now!"

"Hello!" said a deep male voice.

"Dr Dixit?" The urgency in the voice caught him.

"Yes? I am in the middle of a . . ."

"Please listen. I am Ananya Bhatt, Ananya Bhatt, the chief editor of **AFTER TEA** magazine? . . . We had met in Karuna Hospital last week . . . Rajeev drug addiction . . . case?" Ananya was incoherent.

"Look, ma'am, I am in the middle of an important meeting. I cannot give interviews."

"I am not asking for an interview . . . it's, it's my . . . my baby, I am asking to be saved. She has rash all over her body. She is very seriously ill . . . the doctors are unable to diagnose the symptoms . . . I need your help, Doctor! I could not think of anyone else, Doctor. Please, Doctor, don't say no!"

Mrs Verma stood next to Ananya, nodding with tears in her own eyes. She perfectly understood a mother's pain.

"Please! Please! She is ill for almost ten hours now . . . she has high temperature. She has a rash all over her body. She looks very different . . . doctors here are clueless. She is crying non-stop. She did not have a drop of milk for the last seven hours . . . If she is not treated in time, something serious will happen to her! Something serious will happen! It's a mother imploring you, Doctor, please! I need your help." Ananya started to sob.

"How old is she?"

"Ten months"

"Where are you now?"

Ananya gave him the address.

"Sanjeevani? Yes, I think I know. In Kandivali? I am in my clinic. It will take anywhere between half an hour . . . to forty minutes."

"Please come, Doctor, please? I am ready to pay you . . . I am."

The phone went dead.

#

Dr Dixit turned to the patient sitting in front of him. "Continue with the medicines and call if need be. It's an emergency. I need to rush immediately."

Ananya gave Mrs Verma Dr Dixit's number to follow up on him. She saved his number twice in two different names in her mobile. She ran back into the ward and picked up Alia, who by now was tired after continuous crying and could only whimper painfully. Ananya could feel the pain in her own gut as her baby writhed one more time in her arms.

'Please, God, let there be no traffic . . . let Dr Dixit come fast . . . don't let this happen one more time. God!' How she missed Rahul.

The entire team of doctors looked at Ananya with sympathy.

"He is coming. Dr Dixit is coming . . . He will be able to diagnose perfectly. He is an expert in skin ailments . . . I have faith," Ananya blurted out to Dr Malhotra as he looked on clueless!

"We have also asked for the available skin specialist. He is on his way," informed Dr Malhotra. Ananya just rocked her sick baby in her arms.

Dr Dixit was a middle-aged man with thinning hair, married for over thirty years and a father of four children. He was gentle and empathetic, and his long experience had taught him to understand a patient from the body language. Ananya's voice said it all! He needed to rush. He put ignition to his BMW and sped towards Sanjeevani Hospital.

#

It was almost 7.30 when Dr Dixit walked into the special ward for children in Sanjeevani Hospital.

Alia's condition was deteriorating, and the other skin specialist was nowhere in sight.

Dr Dixit nodded stiffly at the doctors on entering the room, gave a wry look towards Ananya, and turned to the sick infant immediately.

He examined her little body carefully for some time; he asked Ananya to hold her while his fingers moved deftly over the baby's skin feeling the rash . . . he pressed some red pimples on the neck and legs without busting them . . . he also extensively examined her tiny torso, neck, and trunk.

He turned to Ananya and asked, "Is she exhibiting small jerking movements?"

"I think so. I am too worried to notice."

"Of course! She has a running nose, does not she?"

"Yes!"

"Did you see this rash before as in sometime before the fever set in?"

"No."

"Does she pass urine lot of times?"

"Yes . . . yes, Doctor, yes!" Ananya said breathlessly.

"Did you administer vaccination for herpes?"

"Herpes? I am afraid I do not under . . ."

"OK! Don't worry. Right now we need to do what we need to . . ."

He turned to the team. "She is suffering from what we call in medical terms as roseola or exanthem subitum, a slight upper respiratory illness with swollen lymph nodes . . . it's caused by herpes virus . . . we need to start the treatments immediately."

The doctors nodded. Dr Malhotra came forward and shook hands with Dr Dixit.

"Give her acetaminophen or ibuprofen (very small dosages)—Mortrin or Advil . . . alternatively . . . and sponge baths are a must . . . every hour . . . administer the medicines thrice a day . . . keep checking on her condition," he spoke to Dr Malhotra in a corner. Both doctors discussed quietly for some time as Ananya rocked her baby. The nurses ran around, preparing for the next sponge bath.

He finally turned to Ananya.

"The fever should vanish in three days along with the rash." He put a reassuring hand on her shoulder . . . "It's a general respiratory disease caused by a virus generally found in infants between six months to two years, which you need not know about. The precautions to be taken later . . . I will brief you."

"OK," Ananya whispered.

"I have directed Dr Malhotra about the treatments . . . if anything, give a call," he said.

"Doctor, your fees! How do I pay now that . . . ?"

"My interview, you remember?" He tried to joke. "We will see later. Don't worry about that. She should be fine once the medicines are administered. Right now she needs you. Please do not hesitate to call me. Docs here will keep me posted about her improvement! I will also find time to visit her."

Ananya thought, 'He is God,' when he left.

Evening turned to night; long shadows fell in the ward. Alia was shifted into a special child room. Mrs Verma followed them like a shadow and waited outside as a loyal friend should. Ananya was clueless about the world.

After about eight o'clock, Mrs Verma came into the room and informed Ananya that she was leaving for home and would be back. Ananya just nodded. She just sat next to the sleeping baby now tucked away with an intravenous that was feeding glucose into her little body. Mrs Verma returned with Mr Verma at 9.30 with a box of vegetable *pulav* for Ananya, which was prepared by Marriamma with care.

"Please eat! You need to be strong for your baby . . . please," Mrs Verma coaxed Ananya.

She force-fed Ananya from a spoon. Ananya could hardly manage to eat a few spoonfuls after the long day's ordeal.

'It breaks my heart to see Alia like this with a big syringe inserted into her.'

"Dear, mothers have to bear all kinds of pains. There is no room for weakness. You see, children are helpless. They are dependent on us." Mrs Verma sighed, "Whether the child chooses to look after a parent is his/her choice later."

Though Ananya was very young, she understood Mrs Verma perfectly.

"Here," she coaxed a spoonful of *pulav* again into Ananya's mouth.

Ananya just pushed it away.

That night, Mr Verma slept on the sofa outside for support.

Sanjeevani Super Speciality Hospital was a 10,000-square-foot ultra-modern facility centre constructed in American style. It boasted of a 2,000-square-feet lush green garden and 200 beds. The walls of the children's ward came alive with wallpapers in pastel colours, replete with Disney characters from movies and books.

It also had a food court, with cuisine available from around the world, a play area for toddlers and kids alike, and guest bedrooms. The long spacious corridors had sofas in multicolours for guests. Each room was made after a theme. The rooms had everything in the pairs: one for the baby and the other for the mom. The bed designs, pillowcases, bed covers, and sheets for the babies matched with the moms'. The only difference was in size.

The theme of Ananya's room was ocean—the wallpapers had mermaids, starfishes and 'Nemos' (the cartoon character) peeking out from huge green water plants; the windows had double curtains. The blue satin curtains remained secure with delicate blue satin ribbons on the side, allowing the sunlight to filter through the white crocheted net curtains. The bathroom had two blue bathtubs, one big and one small; two blue washbasins, one big, another baby size. The shape of the washbasins and tubs was like a fish. There were two blue bathrobes with a variety of sea animals on them with two pairs of soft foamy fabric bathroom slippers with huge maroon stuffed starfishes. Baby and adult brushes in blue with tiny mini-fish carvings and a double-lined toothpaste of maroon and blue, matching with the robes, slippers, and brushes, completed the accessories. The children's ward was a different world altogether.

The week that Alia was admitted, friends and neighbours poured in and took turns to stay the night for support. Ananya was oblivious to anything and anybody. In the evening, during visiting hours between five and seven after two days, Nilesh, Richa, and other team members came to see Alia.

Alia slept most of the time, except when she was sponged and given medicines or before and after a feed. Through the mosquito net, she was faintly visible. Though Ananya's room had a bed for her, she hardly slept in it. When she was tired of watching over her baby or adjusting the bed covers around her or checking the intravenous or the mosquito net, she would drop down tired, with her head on the side in a chair.

One of those days, Vicky came visiting too. As he stood watching Ananya from a corner adjusting the bed covers, trying to coax a bottle of milk, wiping a droplet of saliva from the cherubic little face, gently cooing sweet somethings to the sleeping baby, often checking the limbs, feeling the body for temperature or when nothing was there, just fixing back the mosquito net and watching her baby sleep, he saw something else too—Ananya's connection with Alia! It was live and palpable. The new experience sent ripples down his umbilical cord. He saw a reflection of his own mom in Ananya. As people came and went, he stood there glued to the spot till the visiting hours were over. All through, Ananya was vaguely aware of Vicky's presence, though she did not interact with him.

The next early morning, Ananya stepped out of her room for a cup of coffee. She found Vicky fast asleep on the sofa outside her room in his office formals. He had volunteered to stay the night. She went without disturbing him. On her return, she found the sofa empty.

The checkout time was nine in the morning. Ananya went to the reception to pay the bills. Mrs Verma held Alia and Mr Verma held her bags.

"Room number 207? The bill is 2,67,000."

"What? 2,67,000?"

"I cannot believe this," said Mrs Verma "Two lakh so much for a week?" Her voice trailed off.

Ananya took out her credit card.

"Madam! Your bill is paid!"

"Bill is paid? Who on earth?"

"This is another surprise," rejoined Mrs Verma.

"What happened?" asked Mr Verma.

"Her bill is paid already!" informed Mrs Verma to her husband.

"Who paid it? How is it possible?" Ananya asked, confused.

"One Mr Vicky Arora . . . he paid the bill an hour ago!" the receptionist informed them.

It was a Friday; the small village of Rampur was awake from dawn. The peepal trees sang the songs of winter while the colourful village belles had filled their pots and retreated steps homeward. The village roads were replete with bullock carts, and the farmers were active in the fields. The village looked picture perfect for Bollywood movies. The serene quietness was broken occasionally by the honking of a vehicle that took a wrong path into the village instead of the beaten track! So as the whole village was busy with the daily chores, the local judges were pronouncing a major judgement on a case long forgotten in the old cupboards.

The courtroom was a small, dingy hall, divided into smaller segments with torn curtains on wooden makeshift dividers; a few rickety chairs, tables with broken legs, and tables with torn files was the decor. Dust hung heavily on the furniture like a second cloth, and the cobwebs came down hanging from the ceilings. The walls had a few lizards crawling here and there. The uncleaned floor was dirty with dry mud. The local judge visited it once in a blue moon for some hearing; otherwise the village children used the building as their playground. The stray dogs sat around lazily. Of late, the dingy courtroom was Vicky's destination once a week for the past two months.

On the day of the hearing, the room was cleaned in months by the local sweeper. The magistrate's rickety table and chair were reinstated at the head of the room. A few chairs for the private and government defence lawyers and a few benches were pulled from a nearby school for the guests. Needless to say, nobody turned up for the hearing.

Vicky came out of the courtroom. He coughed and dusted his expensive Ralph Lauren shirt.

He started to walk towards his car that was parked across the street. By now, a small crowd of village children were swarming around it. Some peeped into it, ducking their palms for a clearer view of the insides while others danced in glee around the vehicle, in spite of the repeated reprimands from Mahesh.

Vicky swiftly crossed the street towards his vehicle. He looked rich and conspicuous in the backdrop of the village.

"Vicky Arora, sir? Vicky sir? Sir?" a voice called.

Vicky stopped in his tracks and looked back.

Gaurav was walking towards him along with an old woman. 'She must be Gaurav's mom,' Vicky guessed. The old woman was absent for the rest of the trial but for this.

Gaurav hurried towards him while the old frail woman walked slowly, taking time.

"Thank you, sir! I do not know how to repay your good act, sir! You have a big heart, sir! I really do not know why you did this for me, sir!" Gaurav was full of gratitude and could not express his thoughts evenly as he was emotional. "I am indebted to you for the rest of my life, sir!" He stopped, unable to continue any more.

"OK, OK! It's nothing!" Vicky said carefully, "It's a part of my social service, nothing else."

Now the old lady reached them.

"Sir? Sir! This piece of land had fed our family for many generations. This has the sweat and blood of our ancestors and my husband. A piece of land is a farmer's bread and butter. Sir, his peace of mind. Today my husband's soul will rest in peace. At least I can hold my head high in the village and walk. I will never again cry under the peepal tree. May God bless you, son! I am a poor mother. I cannot give you anything but my blessings."

"They are enough!" said Vicky earnestly.

The frail old woman put a hand on Vicky's head to bless him in the old Indian way.

"If one human being does not help the other, who will?" Vicky said with a smile.

"Sir! Whenever you need any help, please do not forget me. Please call me, sir. I am so very small in station, but this poor person will move the mountains for you."

Vicky was smiling. "Sure, I will."

"You have done a great favour, sir, to us. Sir, now we can walk with our heads held high in the village," the son repeated the mother's words.

"PLEASE don't say that." Vicky reached to open the car door and turned.

"Where do you stay, err . . . ?"

"In the Bhairavi Slums next to the airport, sir!"

"Oh! The same slums, umm . . . next to the Airport . . . I guessed right!"

"Sir?"

"When I read about it in your case file, I felt that the name sounded familiar. I think it is the same place my friend . . ." He stopped.

"What happened to your friend, sir?" Gaurav asked, concerned.

"No, he wanted to relocate the people there. Wanted to build homes for the poor. He is facing some problem, I think."

Gaurav was quiet. Vicky watched his expression change! He spoke carefully.

"As you know, Gaurav, I am deeply involved in social work." Gaurav nodded. "This was also one of the projects for which I wanted to help my friend with homes for the poor. Somehow, the slum dwellers are very adamant to move out, so I gave up. Now I don't know . . ." Vicky pretended to be unhappy as his voice trailed.

"A huge five-star hotel will be built in its place, sir, but what do we get in return?" added Gaurav.

"Then I am right. It is the same place." Vicky continued carefully, "It's people like us who try help the poor to change their lives, but the poor should understand."

The old woman was all ears. "He is right, *beta*," she added.

A tinge of guilt crossed Gaurav's youthful fiery face. Vicky was watching him carefully again. Vicky firmly shook Gaurav's extended hand and bowed down to touch the feet of the old woman. "I need your blessings, *aai*."

The mother had tears in her eyes. She put a feeble hand on Vicky's head and recited some Sanskrit *slok* that spelt 'long life'!

Vicky's BMW sped on to the highway. In the confines of his luxurious car, he leant back comfortably. The past few weeks were very hectic, but they paid off. The litigation lawyer was fantastic; he made a fortune for himself, while A&A had hired him for peanuts. Vicky knew from the beginning that it was only a matter of time before the case would crack and close in his favour. In the history of the village court, it was a landmark of sorts! He scrolled his mobile and came upon a number.

He spoke to someone.

The BMW caught speed towards destination Mumbai. He knew that the slum evacuation will not be met with any opposition now. A slow smile crossed his handsome face. He could see his dream coming true and billions effortlessly falling into his lap.

#

"Please ask him to call back. It's urgent."

"He is travelling, ma'am."

"Please! I need to talk to him."

"He is busy in an important meeting . . . ma'am."

At other times-

"I informed him, ma'am!"

"We are strictly prohibited from disturbing him . . . ma'am!"

"Did you inform him that I am Ananya, the chief editor of *AFTER TEA*? I urgently want to speak to him?"

"I informed him," said his loyal secretary, Stella. "But since he is travelling out of Mumbai to a remote area on an important case, he has strictly instructed me not to disturb him."

Ananya wanted to connect with Vicky after the hospital bill payment incident. Almost a month after that she had no luck.

Ananya, meanwhile, paid Dr Dixit.

"Helping a patient gives me the maximum satisfaction. A smile on a parent's face is priceless to me," he said smiling gently.

"'A stitch in time saves nine, as they say,'" added Ananya philosophically. "You saved my baby's life."

Book III

SUMMER

To save *AFTER TEA*, Ananya's plan was to connect with her readers. For that, she diligently worked on the core principles of truth and simplicity to begin with. Though *AFTER TEA* was circulated only in the high-end business houses, Ananya kept the language of expression very simple and directly addressed the urban lifestyle issues of stress, fitness, health, fashion, beauty, diet, and interiors to speak a few. This approach gave her product a certain newness and magic! Her meticulous planning, eye for perfection, and simple language worked! While the innovative and attractive covers caught the eyeballs, the fire in her stories left a trail. Everyone got a certain something from *AFTER TEA*. On reading it, the stories played in the mind of the readers much after!

#

After the hospital incident, Ananya made it a point to wind off work early to return home to her baby. She strictly followed the doctor's instructions. Alia's colour was slowly returning to her cheeks and so was her vivacious, bubbly nature.

Ananya at first thought of telling her mom about Alia's health and the hospital incident but decided against it as her mom was a hypersensitive patient of high blood pressure.

As Ananya was relaxing with the baby after work one day, her mom called.

"Yes, Ma?"

"*Beta*! What happened to your mobile, it was not ringing? I was trying. Even *bhaiya* was trying several times."

"Sometimes the lines are bad, Ma," Ananya lied. For the most part she had kept the mobile switched off in the past fifteen days. Specially during the days she was in the hospital.

"Here, *bhaiya* is good, and *bhabi* has joined some office. Whole day I am busy running after Bittu and Pinky," Ma informed her, without Ananya asking.

"Moms always have to run around kids, Ma! ALWAYS," Ananya rejoined.

"But before, I was young, now I am getting old," her mom complained.

Ananya did not want to gossip, so she changed the topic, saying, "I am just back from work and unwinding."

"OK, OK, lot of bill for an overseas call, no? I will speak for two minutes more, *beta*. Give the phone to Alia."

Ananya put the mobile on speaker . . . and near to Alia's ear.

"Mamamammammua," Alia responded to her grandma.

"Grandma loves you, umah, umah. Give kissy, kissy," Ananya prompted Alia.

"*Beta*, she might catch some infection . . . tell that servant of yours, *haan*, what is her name, to take care of hygiene. All the time I am worried about Alia in the care of a servant. She might not be supervising well!"

"Ma?" Ananya complained. "I will manage, *na*? Please, this time don't advise. She might feel bad."

Ananya spoke to her mom for some time more, before hanging up.

The upcoming issue was all about homes and interiors. The interviews of celebrity interior designers to 'budget home' interior designers were being included. The idea was to catch the pulse of a wide variety of readers. This was Ananya's eighty-seventh interview in a row in the past year that she joined *AFTER TEA.*

Monday, 20 November 2012, twelve o'clock. Ananya was in the office of Platinum Nests Builder's, Oshiwara, construction site, very near to her office. She took the interview of Mr Atulya himself for a column 'Soft Talk' that she had introduced in the magazine. It was a page dedicated to success stories. There was nothing soft about the column as the stories of success were replete with adventure and risks. The punch lay in the irony of the title.

12.30. Ananya's sandals flipped sideways several times as she balanced on concrete metal bars, pebbles, sand, and cement, while crossing to reach her car parked far outside the building site. She ducked several times to save herself from falling cement, water, and concrete from above. Men and women workers on the site stood watching her in amusement. She jumped several cement puddles to get out of the building.

12.45. She was in her car and put it in gear. She was about to manoeuvre it to the main street when she heard a loud thud. Thinking that she could have hit something, she looked back to discover a ghastly beggarly man thumping on the back window.

She threw an angry glare at him and screamed.

"*Bhago. Kya?*"

Instead of leaving, he came to the driver's window.

"*Kya hai?*" she shouted in Hindi.

The man folded his hands apologetically . . . "*Mafi,* madam . . . *bolna tha,* madam . . . madam . . . *batana hai iske bare . . . mein,* builder, madam . . ."

She kept the car in the driving mode and lowered the window only a little. Ananya looked around frantically. There was no one in the street, and the building site was at a distance. Right now, she needed to get away. The man looked dangerous and dirty and smelt of alcohol. He was also holding the doorknob tightly. 'What must be the alcohol count?' Ananya's journalist mind tried to figure even in the situation she was in.

"*Chodo* door . . . door *chodo,* police *ko bulaungi,*" Ananya shouted.

The man took a step back on hearing the word 'police', still holding the knob.

'Oh God! From where did he descend?' Ananya thought frantically.

"Ma'am! I watch *Saach Ka Samna* and *Crime Patrol* every weekend. Hundreds of cases, ma'am, in Mumbai, of conmen," Richa's voice reverberated in her head. Ananya's immediate reaction was to flee.

'Will not people laugh at me?' she thought. A gutless senior editor running away at the first sign of danger was funny. 'Besides, what kind of an example will I set for my team?' **The best virtue a journalist must cultivate is being fearless at all times. Besides, she wanted to lead by example!** She stood her ground.

"Please, no, madam, forgive me, madam. I am not a bad person, only a worker, madam," the man blabbered. He looked apologetically at Ananya's expression. "*Pariwar*, family, *mera*, madam . . . *mere chote chote bache*, madam . . . worker, madam . . . madam."

"What do you want?" shouted Ananya in Hindi, mustering enough courage and suppressing nervousness. **Another valuable lesson she had learnt was that a journalist needed to look expressionless in the face of the most daunting circumstances.**

"I want to give information."

"About?"

"We poor people are getting fooled, madam . . . working all day for these rich people you taking interview. He fooling journalists, also making a name."

"Who? How do you know that I am taking interview?" shouted Ananya.

"Worker *hoon*, liftman *ne bataya*."

"Why don't you tell your story to the police?"

"*MuJhe koun sunega? Faida nahin.*"

She was here to take the success story of a radical builder . . . now she had another story too of a poor drunkard worker? The life of a journalist was unpredictable. She wanted to laugh and cry at the same time.

Ananya studied the man. He did not look so dangerous as at first. He was not beggarly either, just plain shabby. He was a little drunk. Ananya's curiosity got the better of her. She got an idea.

"*Tumko kuch batana hai to aaoge* office *mein? Yehan nahin.*" . . . That way she could also escape the drunkard, she thought; besides, the place was not right for a talk.

"Office *mein aa jana, yehan nahi,*" she repeated with a movement of her hand.

"Office *mein aaa jaoon, madamji?*" the man said, still holding the door knob.

"*Haan, haan! Aaj 2 baje aa paoge?*"

"*Kahan* office?"

She gave him the address.

"*Haan,* madam, 2 *baje.*" He looked a little sober now.

"If you don't turn up, then we are not going to entertain you again," Ananya said sternly, putting the ignition, and she sped into the street.

One o'clock—Ananya reached office. She quickly ordered a pasta, her favourite vegetarian dish, from the European Kitchen, an upbeat Italian restaurant nearby.

She dialled Nilesh.

Nilesh was at Crystal Juice Centre nearby, having his after-lunch drink.

He frowned as Ananya's number buzzed on his mobile. 'Did ma'am return, or is she calling from the site?'

He placed the juice glass on the counter to take the call.

"*Hann,* ma'am?"

"Where are you, Nilesh?"

"I am outside, madam, at the juice centre."

"I want you to be around in the office at two. I want you to check on someone."

"Is he someone important?"

"No, no. I will brief you once you are in. I want the whole team in the conference room at two. There will be privacy there."

"Yes, madam. Sure, madam . . . did you eat your lunch?" Nilesh asked out of courtesy.

"*Hann*, I have ordered something." Ananya hung up.

#

2.30—Vicky was in the designer's presentation at a posh suburban hotel in town. They were the people competing to design the Palace Hotel of his dreams. For the entire project, he needed to select at least the best 6 of the lot of the 448 applicants from around the world. He had shortlisted the best fifty profiles, out of which ten people had their presentations that day.

After lunching on his favourite Italian food pasta primavera with a host of cooling drinks he slowed down towards the afternoon; besides, not a single design presentation caught his imagination.

3 o'clock—He signalled to his project manager, Vikram, "Is this the last?"

"Yes, sir!"

"How long now?"

"Ten minutes more."

"I have a meeting at four."

3.30—Vicky came out of the conference room and addressed the designers.

"Gentlemen! Please excuse me. I have an important meeting . . . my project manager Vikram will take care of you people for the evening."

The designers from different parts of the globe nodded.

His BMW slid into the posh portico. His driver opened the back door for him.

"Mahesh! Oshiwara . . . meeting *hai* 4 baje, fast!"
"*Haan, sab!*"
The car sped towards the destination.

#

4.30 p.m.—Ananya's destination was home! There was not much traffic, but there were a lot of motorbikes at this time of the day.

'The whole place will come alive in a couple of hours,' she thought. The link road was also skirted with innumerable TV and film production houses, advertising agencies, and private publication houses like hers. She enjoyed driving in the area at this time of the day when there was no traffic but the streets were preparing for the nightlife.

She often bumped into a famous film personality or an upcoming TV star.

'I love being here. I love my work and the media.' She thanked her lucky stars.

She drove for some time, feeling the afternoon breeze in her hair and smelling the street food. She saw to her left, at a distance, the huge hoarding of Platinum Nests, Builders and Developers. It could be also seen from a distance for it was huge. She drove in a pensive mood.

Ananya was not expecting the drunken worker that afternoon, but he landed in the office on time! They were fed with gory stories of Illegal construction sites, how the construction concrete was not solid enough to sustain buildings, and how his daughter had lost her life the previous year as the building they lived in had crumpled. Illegal activities, like drug peddling, too happened in the area after dark! Ananya pushed a strand from her face. 'Was there some truth in the drunkard's story? Or was it pure revenge?' She remembered the inert body of Rajeev. She felt fresh anger brimming! Though Rajeev was recovering, the fear of addiction loomed large on the family. So these were the places for shady activities in the city? Was the drunkard an answer to her prayers, to bring the culprits to book?

Ananya pushed another strand from her brow. 'I will drive for some time around and check this place. There is no harm in it,' she decided, curiosity getting the better of her. She drove into the lane.

She crossed the main office at the entrance to the site.

'The interview of Agastya this morning went off well,' she murmured to herself.

She drove aimlessly for some time, going straight. The lane had many by lanes to the left and right, leading to other buildings under construction in the interiors.

5 p.m.—She came to a lane on her left that looked deserted for the most part. She decided to take it. She drove on the bumpy rough road with tall trees, with branches almost growing into each other; they seemed to be whispering secrets.

'The buildings here are almost ready. That is why, this place is deserted!' Ananya thought.

5.20 p.m.—She drove for some time without a clue of how far she must have driven. The evening advanced, the badly constructed dusty lanes became narrower and were deserted. The tall trees cast long shadows overhead; a few crickets started creaking. The place looked like a plot out of a suspense movie!

She saw a building to her left with a lot of cement pebbles and concrete at the basement.

'It looks deserted.' She had an idea.

'Why not click a few pictures now that I am here? Who knows they might be useful later?'

She stopped her car after crossing the building into a depression in the ground.

'Yes, this angle looks good.' She took out her small hand camera (that she carried everywhere) from her long *jhola* and started clicking. Her camera made ominous noise in the unusually deserted street!

Click! Click! She decided to get out for a better view.

5.40 p.m.—She got out of the car. She checked the street on either side; it looked deserted. She decided to click the concrete that was on the floor.

She inched closer to the entrance gingerly. As it was winter, the days were shorter, and the darkness had already descended. More so in the deserted parts of the city.

The whole place was ominously quiet. Her camera made loud, jittery sounds as she clicked at everything she saw. She felt like a soldier at war, with camera in hand, shooting the enemy. She clicked and moved, clicked and moved further, further, and further. Adrenalin pumping, she walked a few steps further into the building. She came to a depression with a slope. She hesitated. **'Taking risks was one of the biggest qualities a good journalist should cultivate!'** she thought and entered the underground parking, which was under construction, gingerly. A huge mound of sand and cement was visible in the far-off corner. There was no stopping her now. As she came to the mound, she thought, 'Along with the pictures, why not carry the sand samples as well?'

She looked around. The silent car parking with large pillars was dark and desolate. The beams cast shadows like a jigsaw puzzle. She took a deep breath and walked further in towards the rubble.

6 p.m.—She checked the mound on her hinges, thinking. She could not click pictures as there was no light there. She scanned the area. She found a tattered plastic bag and a piece of stray paper. She put some of the mixture in both and pushed it down her pockets.

#

In the bylanes of Oshiwara, a small-time drug pedlar was waiting to start his day in one of the buildings under construction.

At around 6 p.m., he saw a woman align from an I10 car. She removed something from the cloth bag on her shoulder. He edged closer and hid behind a pillar.

'It is a camera!'. He stealthily called a number.

A few words were exchanged. After that, a series of calls followed.

#

"What do you think you are doing?" said a voice from the shadows. Ananya almost jumped to her feet with her speech jammed inside her throat. She willed her legs to move, but they wouldn't! She could see the figure gliding towards her from the shadows.

"I . . . I, errr, lost my way and am here," she blurted to play for time.

"And landed up in an underground parking lot of a building under construction to play in the sand? To fill your pocket with it?"

"Who are you? And . . . and . . . ," she blabbered, mustering courage as her voice shook uncontrollably . . . "I am . . ." She willed some words, but she was frozen with fear! There was a vague feeling of familiarity in the voice!

The voice was coming closer now . . . She started towards the entrance . . . Her legs felt like concrete pillars like the ones supporting the car park of that terribly desolate building . . . they just wouldn't move! Heavy and useless.

She wanted to scream, but her voice wouldn't make a sound. She must have run only a few steps when a vice-like grip came from somewhere and held her wrist.

"Oh help! Save . . ." she screamed without a sound escaping her.

"Before appointing people I need to also check their after-work hobbies I guess?"

"What are you doing here?" she retorted defensively.

"I asked you first!"

"I . . . I am collecting proof for . . ."

"For the magazine story, I guess?" he completed.

"Anyway! You will not understand . . ." She could not bear to see his deep-set eyes from close quarters . . . She pulled her hand away, nervous at the proximity.

"You should know that I never work on a story without a proof."

"Right! What is your story this time? How to mix concrete? Is it some kind of a lifestyle story? Sand and cement?"

How could she explain the gravity and the adrenalin 'pumping passion' she had for collecting proof for her stories? How could a fiery writer make a dry, emotionless, unimaginative, businessman understand her work ethics? Why does he think **AFTER TEA** was making waves? He should have known by now!

She thought of ditching the explanation; instead, she started walking to the entrance. She looked a picture with sand and cement all over her face and clothes. Her hair was dishevelled and her pockets overflowing with concrete mixture. She looked like a kid caught doing mischief.

He wanted to laugh at her but felt chivalrously protective at the same time.

"I need to go home, sir. I have collected what I needed," Ananya said at length with her head held high, trying to muster as much dignity as she could in the condition she was in; she walked to the entrance. He walked with her.

"You did not answer my question," she insisted, breaking the uncomfortable silence.

"What question?"

"About your business in this desolate driveway."

"I was on the fifth floor, meeting the developer for my upcoming project, came to my car, and I saw someone on the heap of sand. At first I thought it must be a beggar. As I came closer, I felt that maybe somebody was stealing something. You can imagine my shock when I see the lady whom I appointed as the chief editor sitting on the rubble and collecting sand. Actually, I wanted to make sure, so I observed you for some time before reacting."

She rejoined, tongue-in-cheek . . . "At first I thought it was a ghost, then I thought it was a stalker, then a goon with a gun, coming to kill me. Then I find that it's the boss in my office in the partly constructed, underground parking." Both laughed.

They walked in a comfortable silence to her car; by now the dusty dull street lights were on and so were some lights in the building above. In her hurry to collect proof, she had missed the lights in the building and the cars parked in the parking lot some distance away! It was almost seven now.

She opened the door to get in.

"I think your tyres are flat," Vicky said.

Both the back tyres of her car were flat; she felt infuriated and drained by now. "All the driving on the bumpy roads!" she said without bothering to explain further. They fell silent for some seconds. Vicky spoke at length.

"If you want, I can drop you home or wherever you need to go. I can ask Mahesh to park your car in the office after getting it repaired, if you have no objection."

She already felt weighed down by the hospital incident and now this? But she had no option in the given circumstances! Besides, this was a wonderful opportunity to ask him about the hospital payments. She scanned the desolate street. The buildings looked sinister and the trees like huge dead giants with tattered clothes hanging on them.

She said at last, "I don't mind taking a lift, but I cannot leave my car in here for Mahesh to pick it!" She did not intend staying a second in a desolate place with a man while he waited for his driver either. She decided fast.

"I will drive down to the main road and wait for you on the left, if it is OK?" Vicky had no problem with that.

Seven o'clock—Ananya drove gingerly down the street that was lit up now with dim electric lights at places from makeshift posts. The flat tyres made ominous noise as the pebbles hit the vehicle disturbing the silence. She had a foreboding feeling of someone following her in the dark! Except her vehicle, nothing was visible behind her, as if she was in a deep dark mine. She pressed the accelerator, manoeuvring the vehicle faster without bothering about the flat tyres or further damage. In a few minutes, she could see the comforting traffic at a distance. She drove on to the road and waited for Vicky.

#

A figure unknown to Ananya was walking in the dark, following her slow-moving vehicle. As she parked her car, it stopped too in the shadows, observing her every move with eagle eyes!

161

#

From where she waited, Ananya could hear the loudspeakers blaring away. She could hear the latest number from *Himmatwala* "*Naino main kajra, kajre mein sajna,*" while from the other direction "*Tanduri murgi hoon*" from the film *Dabang*. The nightlife was catching on. Ananya could see hairstylists at work in gay parlours. She could smell food. Food reminded her of Marriamma. She called home and spoke to her loyal servant for a few minutes. Her familiar voice somehow comforted Ananya after the day's dark adventures. Vicky reached her in his BMW, accompanied by Mahesh, in a while.

"Mahesh was sleeping on the first-floor parking lot," Vicky informed her on reaching the spot.

Ananya got out of her car with the camera and her gunny bag and handed the keys to Mahesh. Vicky instructed him what to do, and they started homewards.

#

The drug pedlar out of business that day for obvious reasons . . . focused on watching from the shadows . . . he inched closer without anybody's knowledge, listening and observing every move of the people he had his eyes on.

As Ananya left with Vicky, he called a number again.

"Dara?" he said in a gruff voice . . . a car number and instructions were given . . .

#

Ananya hopped in next to Vicky. This car was a new add-on to the fleet he had. It zoomed smoothly ahead. Ananya felt as if she was floating in a ship.

"Please put on the seat belt!" Vicky requested Ananya.

"Oh! It is great . . . the car!" she exclaimed.

"It is the latest BMW 7 series," Vicky informed her, wanting to laugh at her expression.

"Comfortable?" he asked after a while.

"Yes, I think I'd like the glass down . . . After all these adventures, I would love some fresh air . . ."

"Fresh air in Mumbai . . . you do not want the AC?"

"No."

He pressed a button with no further ado, and the glass came down on Ananya's side.

"I think you also like it. I saw your windows open the first day I stepped into your cabin," Ananya said at length.

"I forgot to ask where I need to drop you," Vicky asked instead.

"In Kandivali. You will have to take the highway, Western Express Highway."

He nodded.

Outside life had started in full swing; the traffic was moving at a slow pace . . . several cars were edge-to-edge, competing for space; some auto-rickshaw drivers inched their way in between the vehicles . . . The bikers drove through the gaps . . . Then there were BEST buses . . . that came from everywhere and anywhere . . . The drivers drove recklessly, brushing other vehicles on the side ramming into them, bumping from behind, or missing them by inches . . . Miraculously, there were no accidents. Women beggars asked for alms with babies in makeshift baby carriers made out of *dupattas*; loudspeakers blared from street corners . . . adding to the commotion. An ambulance was stuck in it too; with continuous blaring of the siren, it could edge only a little ahead . . . Life on the roads in Mumbai was erratic and crazy.

"Imagine if somebody in it is serious, he will surely die till he reaches the hospital." Ananya observed.

"True!" A stray dog crossed the road quickly, saving it's life, while a cow with a broken leg stood between the vehicles, chewing cud, oblivious to the commotion.

Ananya just moved her head . . . "God!" . . .

Vicky smiled, "This is India."

"I guess," she smiled. "There is so much variety everywhere even in the traffic . . . and commotion and noise."

Vicky laughed.

"You miss all this when you stay abroad . . . it is so different in the US . . ."

"You lived in the US? Which part" Vicky asked, interested.

"California."

"Where exactly in California?"

"488, Ocean View Boulevard, California, just opposite the Pacific Ocean." She could not continue more . . . her mind went to the beautiful apartment she lived, in the United States, opposite to the Pacific Ocean. She felt the pang of loss one more time.

He did not know much of California . . ."I studied my MBA there, in the US," he said.

"Really? In California?"

"No, in New York! . . . NYU Stern School of Business."

"Great!" She had never heard of it, but she nodded.

They came to a signal. A woman sat on the footpath, nursing her baby under the street lamp while another made a basket out of cane. Several men sat smoking around; some of them had plastic wares and comics that they sold at the signal. A small girl in an overgrown muddy frock came to the window to beg; a baby was fast asleep in her arms.

Ananya just shuddered. Vicky pressed the button, and the glass came up half on her window. Ananya watched the girl making pathetic faces at her. She pulled out a ten-rupee note and passed it on to her. Within seconds, more beggar children swarmed at Ananya's window. That very moment the traffic lights turned green, and they moved ahead.

Vicky was laughing. "This is the real India. The rich and the poor live side by side."

"True!" Ananya laughed.

"How long were you in the US? Were you studying there?" Vicky asked, changing the topic.

"No, I got married and went to stay there . . . I stayed for over three years . . . sir!"

"Oh! That is great . . . don't call me sir . . ."

"I think I work for you, and I want to keep it professional."

He frowned. "It is OK to call me by my name. Even in big organisations, people call each other by names so . . . ?"

After he learnt about Ananya's stay abroad, Vicky got more curious to know about her. As he didn't want to be prying, he refrained from asking further personal questions and concentrated on driving.

Ananya continued, "I got married to Rahul. He was a Web designer and an architect. We shifted base to the US. I returned after my husband passed away in an accident."

"I am really sorry about that."

"I have a baby . . . I have wonderful memories."

"Yes, of course! I know!"

Now that the topic of the baby came up, naturally Ananya asked, "I wanted to ask why you paid the hospital bills?"

"I just felt like . . ." His voice trailed.

"You just don't pay 2,67,000 because you feel like. Besides, I am not a poor woman in need of money."

"I never said that. Where I come from, money is not so important but timely help is. I felt that you were alone taking care of a toddler, and when I checked on the bill, it was quite a sum so the manners asked for . . ."

"For paying 2,70,000 . . . It is more than manners . . . and you need not have checked on the bills . . . I mean, it was uncalled for."

Vicky had nothing to say on that . . . He just said, "Maybe that is how I was brought up."

'It is how rich you are,' Ananya thought but said aloud, "I agree, but I insist on paying the money back. I cannot accept it."

"I love helping people. I thought you will thank me," he said, disregarding her rejoinder . . .

"Look, I am thankful, but it was not necessary. I was trying to contact you all these months, but you were inaccessible.

"I know. I know. Please do not be in a hurry . . . just pay when you are most comfortable. Take your time . . ."

"No, I will give it back this very week. I would have paid the hospital anyway . . . and I am comfortable . . ."

"Suit yourself." Vicky did not want to argue with the fiery woman next to him.

"Thanks a lot for everything . . . Vicky! For staying the night, for paying the bill. It was not necessary, though," she said again. "From where you come, it is much below your station to sleep on a sofa . . ." Her voice trailed . . . "Out of your way . . . but thanks."

"Thanks accepted!"

"I was totally oblivious to the world those days . . . I am thankful to all the people who helped me through."

"You said it," he said, joking. "Now do you understand my sentiment? Am I allowed to say something? Make an observation maybe?"

"Yes?"

"You have an amazing connection with your baby . . ."

"Oh, really? I never thought about that. All moms just have a connection."

"I just felt something come over me when I saw you with her. You reminded me of my mom . . . No, I am not saying that you look old . . ." he joked again. "That connection, that touch, so real."

Ananya nodded. Her eyes became moist; she turned her face away to the traffic. The breeze from the window was in her hair, blowing it softly.

Vicky looked at her from the corner of his eye; her hair often fell all over her face. She made an effort to push it behind her ears. But it found its way back! There were traces of sand in it and on her clothes. Her trousers were a little muddy and crumpled too, with the rubble she had filled at the site falling out of her pockets. She was watching the traffic, and as the wind blew gently, she pushed yet another stray strand back from her face. Vicky just moved his head in amusement.

"You need to empty your pockets, I think." He pointed out, trying not to laugh.

"I have . . . I had collected the rubble in a plastic, now it is in my bag," she said seriously. "I want to give it for some kind of scrutinisation."

"Oh! That's great!" He wanted to laugh at her childish single-minded determination and again controlled himself in time. He fell back, observing her again as the vehicle moved slowly in the heavy traffic. The large off-white shirt buttoned till the neck gave her a studious look. She looked like a student returning home after soiling her clothes in the school playground. He suppressed a smile again. He could not but observe how unassumingly simple yet intelligent she looked. Her large luminous grey-brown eyes, sharp nose, flawless white skin now flustered was shown in the lights from the street. Her lips turned slightly at the corners, looked as if she was questioning the whole world. He just shook his head, a little incredulous. She on the sand heap was more amusing than anything he had witnessed in years. It suddenly occurred to him how different she was from the women he knew!

Though Ananya had lost all her pregnancy weight, she never cared to dress up for herself. All her energies were focused on her work and Alia.

'Dressing up seems to be the last thing in the world for her,' he thought, amused. 'But there is a certain something about this woman. She will never go unnoticed even in a crowd!'

They came to a turning on the S. V. Road. A huge structure with tall carved pillars was in view to the right; the traffic was a little slow as the cars were pulling into the building here. The guards were extensively checking every vehicle.

"This is the new Marriot," said Vicky. "They have built it after the ancient Indian historical monuments. The whole structure looks ancient."

"I don't know about the Indian structure, but it looks Greek, and I love old structures simply because they have a history to it," rejoined Ananya.

"True! The other Marriot in Juhu also looks Greek. I love everything that is Greek and Italian. They serve great pasta here, in this Marriot," Vicky added.

Ananya thought, 'I love pasta too.'

"There seems to be some awards function going on here today," remarked Vicky.

"Seems to be," she agreed.

Their car stopped near the gates in the traffic at a distance. Ananya saw several starlets in skimpy outfits alighting from the big cars. The skimpily dressed women seemed to spill everywhere. Glamour was the quotient for the evening . . . Their BMW moved ahead.

"This is India, the modern and the conservative live amicably together," Ananya stated aloud.

"Very true. I know where it came from."

They both laughed.

'I should take some celebrity interviews for **AFTER TEA,**' thought Ananya. 'I would love to write about glamour some day!' She saw a couple of cars with the label PRESS on them going in. She felt elated. They came to the Western Express at last; the traffic was slow but steady.

Ananya observed Vicky.

'He has rich Aryan features, dusky and dark . . . women must be mad for him . . . He is not like those rich, reckless, irresponsible men . . . he is "grounded" . . . yes! "Grounded" is the word for him.' She decided.

He caught her looking at him. She turned crimson.

"I was wondering why you did not join Bollywood," she asked. "Most rich handsome guys do," she added, covering up for herself.

"I had other aspirations . . . I wanted to make Mumbai the business capital of the world by building world-class structures. That is a bigger aspiration, I suppose!"

"Oh! True."

"As we are on the topic of building and constructions, I would like to know your interest in sand and cement too," he joked.

"I am not interested in that." She recounted her experience of the morning about how she had met the drunkard and how she got curious after she heard his story and finally landed at the construction site.

"What were you doing there yourself?" Ananya asked Vicky, changing the topic as she felt ridiculous at her own adventure now.

"I told you I had gone to meet the builder in his office for the upcoming project. Then he took me to see the interiors to get a rough idea as it (the building) was almost ready."

He added further, "You should be careful in venturing out alone. Most of the work in a small set-up of a publication like ours is done by the staff, but you need not jump everywhere and fall into trouble. Are you going to do a story on it?"

"Aaah! No, I am not because it does not fit anywhere into the theme. Not at least so far. Maybe a soft supporting story . . . maybe, don't know."

"Then?"

"I thought of helping the guy find some justice. I don't know. Maybe I wanted to find answers to several questions myself!" Her voice trailed.

Vicky was impressed by her idea but advised, "Please do not venture in the future on your own."

She nodded. They fell silent. Ananya sat back and relaxed. She felt surprisingly comfortable in his company, given the fact that he was almost a stranger to her. She thought, 'We are chatting like old friends!'

Their car in the traffic was moving at a snail's pace. On the footpath next to them were a group of children with boxes of strawberries. As they stopped at the signal, a child came up to her with a box. Taken in by the rich colour of the fruit, she decided to buy it. Suddenly she saw several boys with similar boxes of fruit on the footpath next to them. In one corner, away from the gaze of the public, a ruffian was cleaning the box of fruit for sale. He was using his shirt sleeve and something else too. Ananya's eyes popped out with detest!

"Go away," she shouted to the boy standing at her window. "He is putting his spit to clean the fruit," she said in disgust.

Vicky laughed.

"I am observing all this because my windows are down today, ma'am," he joked again. "Otherwise, I unwind with my glasses up, AC on, and music," he chuckled. "I have this latest CD . . . 'The Fifty Retro Songs to Hear While You Are Alive'. Do you want to hear?" he asked Ananya, still laughing.

She moved her head. "My home is nearing."

They came to the Times of India signal.

'This is the longest,' she muttered under her breath.

A small bedraggled boy with bunches of yellow, red, and white roses came to her window.

"Please, madam, take, madam," he said in broken English.

"These kids speak English?" she laughed. Vicky joined her.

The other kids with bunches came to her window too. She selected a bunch of white rosebuds for her altar at home. They looked pure and divine.

"At least they must not be putting spit on them. They seem to be fresh," she observed while buying. As they crossed the signal, a child vendor removed some of the outer petals to expose the fresh buds within, before running to the next vehicle.

"Oh God! Atrocity," Ananya cried. "They must be selling these flowers for days, fooling people."

Vicky just laughed, moving his head again.

The rest of the journey was fast. Vicky shared with Ananya his childhood stories and the city life he grew in, while she spoke to him about her mom and papa. She spoke about the dog collars that her mom wore, which scared her to bits. That was also the reason why she was freaked to take up teaching as a career! Vicky laughed heartily all through.

"In my childhood, I saw Pop work continuously on building designs. I really admired him. I never had the inclination towards the construction business, so after my MBA, I forayed into restaurants and investment banking. Now that Dad is getting old, I stepped in. I love it like nobody's business. I want to make A&A the best! I want to bring the world to my favourite city. After we finish with the Mumbai Palace Villa, it is going to happen!"

Ananya nodded. "My papa worked in a bank too. I understand a little about investment banking myself."

"Oh great!" said Vicky, again suppressing an amused smile.

"Now he is no more. After my pop passed away five years back, me and my bro take turns taking care of mom."

"Where is your brother staying?"

"In London. He is a banker too . . . I think you guys will get along well," Ananya said.

"Yes, why not . . . sure! Get him to meet me when he is here," Vicky rejoined.

By now the lights and buildings of Thakur Village were visible.

"You have to take a turn to the right. I will walk home from there . . . since I need to pick up stuff . . ."

"OK!"

"What is a good time to talk to you?" Ananya asked. "I was planning to give the cheque."

"Oh! Yes, of course, the cheque." Vicky shrugged. "Whenever during the office hours?"

"I was trying all these days in the office hours to reach you," she said, getting out of the car, complaining.

Vicky bent down a little to talk to her through the window.

"In that case, you can drop in at my place." He went on to add quickly, "My parents will be around, someone is always around. You are most welcome."

"I will try. Thanks for being so humble . . . Thanks for taking care of my car, for this lift, for everything. I really appreciate it," Ananya added and walked away without looking back.

\#

Vicky pressed the button near the driving wheel. The glass came up. He switched the AC on and slipped the CD into the player. While the music played, he waited on the spot for some time watching Ananya. When was the last he laughed heartily? When was it that he was himself and happy? When was it that he enjoyed the company of a woman without worrying about the repercussions? He reflected on the eventful evening. If he had not met her, he would be in a bar by now, having a drink or entertaining some boring house guests or spending the time planning for the next day! 'She made the evening so refreshingly enjoyable in a simple way!' He waited till she turned a bend and disappeared! This woman never failed to intrigue him. He put the car in Ignition, smiling.

\#

9.30 p.m.—Ananya walked from the car to the nearest general store. Halfway through, the strap of her sandal gave way. Effortlessly, she picked both the sandals in one hand and quickly walked barefoot on the rough, patchy road, balancing her gunny on the shoulder. She was attracting the attention of the passers-by, with slippers in hand, sand in her hair, and dirty clothes. She limped to a grocery store and bought brown bread for breakfast. The men in the shop gaped while the women looked on as if she were a rape victim. Ananya was past seeing anything.

'It's been a long day,' she thought. 'I will just take a warm shower and plonk on the bed.' The thought of warm food, bath, and Alia brought her joy.

#

A black Maruti Omni was parked on the road near the general store; the glass came up as Ananya passed. Someone had followed her all the way without her knowledge.

"Ananya madam, editor?" the gruff male voice said without a preamble.

Ananya immediately felt nervous. The voice was unusual, gruff, and sounded nasty. The man spoke in broken colloquial English.

Most of the calls from the board to her were filtered. She did not speak to people without prior appointment. This came as a surprise!

"Yes!" Ananya said uncertainly "Who the?"

"Madam . . . just listen . . . you at the site yesterday?"

"What? Which?"

"*Haan ke na*?" he said in Hindi this time.

"I do not understand?"

"*Haan ke naa*?" He bullied. "I am asking you to stay away from the area . . . if you go to the construction site again . . ."

"Who the hell is this? . . . Are you threatening me?"

"I am only requesting you, madam. Don't ask questions . . . just listen."

"Who is this? How did you get this number?"

"Listen! . . . Madam, no questions. Just follow whatever I am telling you, madam! It is not difficult, madam, to find numbers . . . You are thinking you are great woman, you running this country?" shouted the man bossily.

"I am . . . err . . . I will call the police . . . It is not legal . . . Were you following me or . . . ?" Ananya said, shaking.

"You ask too many questions . . . just listen, stay away from the area . . . nothing will happen to you. Stay away from yesterday's construction site. I repeat, stay away, you will be safe, *kya*?" He spoke in Mumbai *tapori* language now . . . "You will be in trouble, big trouble, if you don't." The phone went dead.

Ananya sat there for a long time, trembling; the ground under her felt wobbly.

She had all types of mixed feelings first. She thought of calling the police and telling her team, raising an alarm. She ran through the conversation in her mind many a times.

"If you stay away, you will be safe" the words rang in her ears again and again.

A Valuable lesson she had learnt in the short span of her career was to stay calm to take right decisions. If after the previous day's misadventure Ananya had decided to take it slow in finding the truth, she was not going to now. She was boiling from within for not able to put the words back in the man's mouth! She was hell-bent on bringing the B@#$%^&@ to book! She was not going to chicken out and give up. After considering all the options, she decided to act with tact and fast!

She picked the Mumbai Yellow Pages, came upon a number, and dialled.

A voice at the other end responded . . . "Good morning! This is *Mumbai News* how may I help you?"

"May I speak to the chief editor . . . Mr Allen d'Cruz?"

"Who is on the line please?"

"This is the chief editor from the lifestyle magazine *AFTER TEA* . . . Ms Ananya Bhatt."

"*AFTER TEA*?" the woman repeated to confirm.

"That's right!"

"Just a moment please!" The woman put her on hold.

A male voice with a somewhat British accent came on the line. "Chief Editor Allen."

"I am Ms Ananya Bhatt, chief editor *AFTER TEA* magazine."

The guy jumped at the female voice. "How may I help you, errr?"

'The foreigner cannot pronounce my name for the life of him,' thought Ananya angrily.

"I have a sensational story for you."

"Sensational?" he repeated.

"Yes! I cannot use it, as ours is a lifestyle magazine, so I am passing it on. The leads are true."

"You the editor?" said the British accent seemingly least interested in the story.

"Yes! I thought of briefing it to a newspaper as you guys are the voice of Mumbai."

Before she could complete he asked, "How do you plan to send the story? Meet me in person?"

'Is the jerk sitting there to find a date or something?' She was very angry after the creepy call and this man was infuriating her more!

"I will ask my team to mail you the story with the pictures," said she, cutting him short. "Most men in the mainstream papers are womanisers," Amanda had warned her. 'He sure is one. All are f#&*%* bastards,' Ananya thought. By now she was seething in anger!

"We will mail it as fast as we can!" she rejoined crisply. There was no response.

"Hello?"

"Sure!" He sounded really disinterested. He nearly seemed to have hung up!

'Bloody jerk!' thought Ananya again. She spoke, swirling her words, flirting a little. "You have a great day, Mr Allen. In all fairness, I know you will go to the root of the story. Justice will be done."

He sounded enthusiastic again at Ananya's swing in the voice. "I will definitely. If need be, I will call you to find out more, err!"

She cut the call.

#

After hanging up, Ananya thought of calling Vicky for two reasons, one to ask for an appointment to return his money and second to inform him about the threatening call. She was about to call Vicky when her phone rang. It was an unknown number.

"Hello?" she said gingerly.

"Is this the chief editor of **AFTER TEA**?" said a sweet, eloquent female voice.

"Yes! Who is this?" asked Ananya.

"This is the chief editor of *Starbust* magazine. Ms Sharbani Goswami."

"Hello, ma'am," responded Ananya. "Do I . . ."

"No, you do not know me, but I took the liberty of calling you," the lady responded before Ananya could finish her line. "This is Ananya I am speaking to, isn't it?"

"How may I help you, ma'am?" Ananya kicked herself for copying Mr Allen's style. "We as journalists are always in service, tell me?" she said explaining herself.

The lady at the other end laughed.

"That's so true! I reciprocate ditto! For some time now, I had felt like connecting with you to congratulate you for the great job you are doing with *AFTER TEA*."

"That's great, thank you!"

"I had come across your magazine in one of the coffee shops of Taj Palace Delhi and since then I became a fan. I love the choice of topics, the way the stories run, pictures designing, everything about it."

"Wow! That's a huge compliment. Especially coming from you!" Ananya patted herself on the back!

"I loved the alternative healing and meditation that you carried in this issue," the lady said. "I feel everything that you include is foolproof and first-hand."

"You are embarrassing me. You are the one who is an expert. Everybody knows that *Starbust* is the number one film magazine doing the rounds," Ananya said with humility.

"Within no time yours will be the best lifestyle magazine doing the rounds too," Ms Sharbani predicted.

"Do you have interest in editing film magazines by any chance?"

"I never thought of that, ma'am. I don't think I have the experience too."

"Oh, please don't call me ma'am. Call me Sharbani," She said, adding, "If you ever think of quitting the present job, you have ours. People will do anything to work with *Starbust,* you know! We, on the other hand, always are on the lookout for people like you having immense potential! My offer is open and you can take up editing it any time you wish to change. Just let me know in advance!"

"Oh! that is amazing, Sharbani. It's an honour, really!" Ananya said, surprised. "I've never thought of editing film magazines though. Right now, I am quite content editing *AFTER TEA*."

Sharbani said, "Please feel free to walk in if you change your mind. We are looking for people now. Congratulations once again!"

"You made my day. Thanks a million. You have a great day too!"

"All the best!" said the woman, and the line went dead.

Ananya sat there for a long time, basking in the glory of the words spoken by Sharbani Goswami. She felt elated and proud.

Two people, two strangers, one made her feel elated, and the other sick on the same day! 'Life is diabolical,' Ananya reflected.

Ananya finally called Vicky that very day.

Vicky was in the first-class lounge of Singapore Airlines Mumbai. He was flying to Frankfurt, Agatti Islands, to meet several international architects for his upcoming project. This was an afternoon flight direct to destination Agatti.

He walked to the food counter for a cup of afternoon coffee. He was dressed in semi-formals. He had a white full-sleeved shirt on with dark brown-beige Arrow Jackson informal trousers and Born-rich kick sneakers. His dark features looked imposing yet subtle in the attire.

As he was pouring himself black coffee in a huge mug, his phone rang.

It was an unknown number.

"Hello?" he said.

"Hello!" said a female voice gently. "This is Ananya Bhatt."

"Oh, Ananya! How are you?" A smile crossed his face.

"I am doing great! How about you?" Ananya lied; she was all jitters after the creepy call.

"Great!"

"I wanted to see you regarding the cheque I wanted to give!" she said directly, and added, "Hope I am not disturbing you?"

"No, not really! I am on my way to Frankfurt to catch a flight. I am at the airport."

"Oh!" She decided against telling him about the call now that he was travelling; instead, she asked "When will you return back? When can we meet?"

"Umm! I will be back on Thursday night. We can meet sometime, maybe umm, say Saturday?"

"Saturday?"

"Yes! At my Nariman Point office? We do not work on Saturdays as you know."

"Yes, we also don't work on Saturdays," she joked back, and added, "Actually Saturdays are a little difficult for me, ummm, what about Friday? Little early, maybe around four?"

"Oh! Friday post lunch should be good, but I am not confirming. Need to check." Then he added "If I do not have any prior appointments, then we are meeting at four, Friday."

"That's so nice of you, if we can."

"You need not be so formal, Ananya."

"Then it is four o'clock this Friday?"

"Will an SMS do? I will SMS you after checking my appointments."

"That will be great! I will wait for your SMS. You have a safe flight. Oh yes, I have sent a copy of this month's *AFTER TEA*. Please go through it!"

"OK, you be safe," he said before cutting the call.

"Sir, if you like to read, we have some magazines," an attendant at the lounge said. He pointed to a magazine shelf on the far-right corner of the lounge.

"Thank you! I will."

Vicky went to the shelf with the cup of coffee and leafed through a bunch of magazines.

A familiar name peeked at him out of the many. *AFTER TEA*.

He was excited; he took the copy. It was that month's edition, which Ananya was speaking about!

He went back to his place with his coffee mug and the magazine. He skipped through several pages. It seemed quite enriching.

#

After a while, Vicky's flight was announced. He started walking towards the entrance with his laptop and the Voi Jeans jacket slung on his arm.

He passed a magazine store on his way to the gate and saw a familiar name peeking out of the many on display . . . *AFTER TEA*.

'I will buy one on my way back,' he thought, excited.

He passed through the VIP departure gates meant for only first-class passengers. Vicky loved to fly by Singapore Airlines. In first class, they had cubicles for each passenger that allowed them to relax and work. If he was not working, he was entertained by countless movies. Food and service was always extraordinary.

As he entered, a woman with a hourglass figure wearing a *sarong kebaya* came up to him.

"Welcome aboard Singapore first class, Mr Vicky," she addressed him by his name.

"I am Ah Lam. I am your official attendant on the flight."

"Thank you!"

Ah Lam offered him newspapers, magazines, headphones, a hot towel, an amenity kit, socks, eyeshades, Givenchy pyjamas, and the menu for the night.

In a few minutes, the flight took off into the clouds. Vicky fell back on his seat. He kicked his kick sneakers, put up his feet, and moved the warm towel gently on his face. After a while, Ah Lam came to take away the discarded towels and tucked the blanket properly, which he had pulled around in her absence.

He could hear a woman ask the hostess in attendance, "How do you maintain such a slim figure? What do you do for it?"

"I walk up and down whole day attending to the guests, nothing else. That keeps me slim."

'Women will be women!' Vicky mused.

He adjusted more comfortably on his seat and scanned through the magazines given to him and finally settled on one. Ah Lam came back with a trolley, smiling.

"What would you like to drink, sir?"

He asked casually in return, "What is this magazine? I never saw it before."

"Oh that? It is **AFTER TEA**, the best lifestyle magazine introduced recently on board."

"Oh!"

She went on, "Specifically on demand from customers. It is available only for the first-class and business-class passengers of Singapore Airlines."

"Oh, that is great! I will go though it. Seems interesting."

"It is, please go through the article on meditation, Mr Vicky. It is awesome! I tried. It works."

"Oh, really? A midnight dream please?" he said. She poured out his request.

Sipping a drink at 30,000 feet, he read *AFTER TEA* word by word. 'It is unputdownable,' he thought.

He went through the articles till he had read every word! He came to the last page. The large grey-brown eyes bore into him, smiling. Without his doing, he started to smile! Ah Lam served dinner. Before closing his eyes for the night, he skipped to the last page; the large grey eyes stared back! Vicky looked eagerly forward to that Friday.

He got down at Agatti the next day, and the first thing he did was to confirm the Friday's appointment with Ananya. He could not wait to see her.

#

AFTER TEA was making waves in the market. It was 'the magazine' in demand in pubs, high-end restaurants, coffee houses, airport lounges, and international airplanes. It had something for everyone. From the intelligent to the dull, the old to the young. Ananya's name was being taken with respect in the industry; her personal mail ID and the professional mail ID overflowed every day with congratulatory messages from friends, colleagues, and the industry bigwigs. Heavy pay packages were offered every day from her competitors to join them.

'This is the greatness of being a journalist. The whole world knows you, without you going anywhere,' she told herself. She worked harder to meet the deadlines. She worked consistently on new strategies for circulation, distribution, and marketing, to fulfil the hunger of her readers. She left no stone unturned to unearth the truth for the stories. There was no stopping her now. THERE WAS NO LOOKING BACK!

"Right now, I am content editing *AFTER TEA*. No, thank you, sir. No, thank you, ma'am. I am not interested. I will consider it later." She refused a lot of offers every week!

'My baby is growing well. I am doing what I want. Who knows the future? Right now, no changes for me,' she told herself every time someone rang her with a job offer!

Ananya's phone rang again. 'This must be the 999th for the day,' she thought exasperatedly that afternoon after speaking to Vicky at the airport.

"Hello?" she said in low tones as she was editing a copy.

"Aim ie speaking to Ms Ananya Bhatt, the editor of **AFTER TEA**?"

"Yes? That's right!" 'Who is this loony now?' thought she. The voice had a heavy South Indian accent.

"I am Mr Swaminarain from the National Journalists' Association of India, maidam!" said the heavy accent.

"What can I do for you, sir?" Allen's style lingered on.

Ananya was planning to make 'what can I do for you?' the signature line for **AFTER TEA**. She smirked at herself, at the thought.

"Ma'am, you have been shortlisted for the Best Editor's Award."

Ananya sat up.

"What?"

"Since last two years, National Journalists' Association has introduced an award called as The Best Editor. We select and shortlist five best editors for the annual awards ceremony. *AFTER TEA* tops the list of lifestyle magazines, and your name is shortlisted for the Best Editor's Award along with four others."

"How did you zero in . . . I mean on . . . on me? I mean, what is the criteria? How did you?" Ananya asked all at once.

"Our association conducts survey on two levels."

"One is the general, other specific. The general survey is based on the criteria of growth of the magazine. Your magazine increased its circulation from 2,000 to 300,000 copies in this year alone. That is remarkable, considering the market value of any upcoming publication. In the specific category, we take into account the language, authenticity of stories, design, credibility of features, and other finer aspects that go into making a publication what it is. The credit goes to the editor as he/she is the whole and soul without a doubt! We conducted a survey of *AFTER TEA* for preferability by the clients over other lifestyle magazines and the score was 9.999 on a scale of ten!"

"Wow! Is it?" Ananya could not speak further.

"Now," the heavy accent was saying . . .

"You will have to attend a personal interview, which will be conducted in the presence of our board and a special jury on 7th September, eleven o'clock. We will mail you the details of the award and the interview in a short while."

"Special jury? I . . . err . . ." Ananya could not continue.

"It will consist of eminent people, people . . ." he repeated dramatically . . . "like famous writers, editors, film personalities, models, sportspeople, and politicians invited to interact with the candidates to understand . . ." The accent stopped for effect. "To understand the vision of the achiever, maidam."

"Oh, what is this award? I mean can you come again please? I did not, I am afraid . . . hear it properly . . . I . . ."

"It is the National Award for the Best Editor," the south accent spoke before she could continue.

"It's quite sudden. I never thought . . ." Ananya's voice trailed as she was overcome by emotion.

The voice had a 'respectable smile' "Everything in life is sudden, *na*, madam? Oh! Yes, I forgot, we are recommending your magazine's name for an international award too. We will intimate you about it later. Very few magazines from India are accepted for international awards. But we are very confident about *AFTER TEA*. It will definitely get international acclaim very soon!"

Ananya had no words . . . she just said, "Thank you," before the phone went dead.

She sat there for a long time, reflecting on the call, and pinched herself several times to make sure she was alive. Was it true? Or was it a dream? Whatever it was, it was unexpected and 'happily huge'!

The huge bungalow on the Marine Drive was at the edge of the Arabian Sea; The bungalow was owned by Mr Balraj Arora. For three generations, this ancestral home was a landmark now; the huge mansion always enjoyed the sunshine and the sea breeze and constant attention of passers-by. Mr Balraj Arora was a builder by profession. In his golden years, the seventy-year-old had given up work to enjoy life with family and friends.

During his long years of working life, he had learnt two things—to respect good people and to appreciate talent.

On that Friday morning, he walked down the alabaster stairway to the living room. Ramu, their loyal servant, opened the doors to the garden and moved aside the long curtains for the view.

Mr Arora sat down on the cushiony sofas, watching the morning activity in his huge gardens. His vast sea-facing garden had a crystal clear pool that glimmered in the morning sun.

Ramu asked Mr Arora "*Saheb, chai?*"

"*Haan.*"

The squirrels went up and down the trees while the parrots chattered merrily. The tiny birds flew around and caught tiny worms from the grass. The ocean in the front looked vast.

The night before, Vicky had returned from Agatti.

He left a few books and papers on the living room table. The senior Arora looked for the day's newspaper. He picked a magazine in the newspaper's absence.

He started to read. That day he forgot his newspapers; the magazine was **AFTER TEA**.

It was the Friday afternoon Ananya was preparing to wind off early.

Her phone rang. It was Vicky.

"Hi, I was just preparing to leave." Vicky just felt happy at the very sound of her voice again.

"That's great. Do you know the venue of our meeting has changed?"

"I did not know tha . . . has it?" Vicky loved the way she reacted and her 'sweet shrill' voice, always quick! He realised how he had missed it since their car drive.

"Yes, now it is, my place."

"Your place?"

"You know, there is a slight twist of plans, and now my parents also want to meet you."

"They want to meet me? Your parents? Why on earth? Oh!" Her voice trailed nervously.

"Yes! You see, like the whole world, they have also become your fans," he rejoined, smiling to himself.

"Oh, that has like how did like . . . ?"

"Like, I will tell you how, when you are here. Join us for a cup of coffee."

"Now? I . . ." Ananya was uncertain. Alarm bells started ringing in her mind. Could she trust someone as rich and new as Vicky? "*Crime Patrol,* ma'am, cannot trust anyone nowadays." Richa's voice reverberated in her mind. Besides, what was she to do with that 'flutter feeling' in her stomach she experienced every time he called or spoke to her? Now he wanted her to meet his parents?

"I don't have your address. Besides, I am not dressed for a formal meeting," she said in a vain attempt of dissuasion!

"I will SMS you the address. Besides, don't bother about the dress. My parents love informal people!" he rejoined quickly like her.

"I will be there same time."

A slow smile crossed Vicky's face 'Dressed?' He remembered the rubble and the sand. Dressed? He laughed to himself. The truth was he had missed Ananya's verbal repartees, intelligent unassuming comments, and her characteristic easy style. He was happy she was coming home. He was happy he would be meeting her again! He was simply happy because he was happy after a long time!

#

"Are you mad?" Amanda said.

"I am not. You know that."

"You infuriate me really, Ananya. A guy like Vicky asks you out and you deny? You must be out of your mind!"

"Really?"

"Yes, you are! Any woman will hand her heart out to just go out with him. Are you mad to reject him?"

"He did not propose to me, by the way. He just asked me out, and I refused. What is so mad about it?"

"You are a nut! . . . If he asks someone else out? If he falls in love in the meantime with someone then?"

"Then? Let him. Besides, I am sure he must be asking a lot of women out. I am sure he is not sitting idle, twiddling his thumbs, and if he does fall in love, in the meanwhile, with someone—and I am sure he will never with me—then that was how it was supposed to be!"

"Then that is how it was supposed to be!" Amanda mimicked her. "Suit yourself, mad girl."

"I don't want to talk about it . . . I should not have told you about it . . . he just asked me out casually, and I sensed it was not right to go out . . . kind of fishy . . . actually uncomfortable!"

"Great, you always smell fish everywhere."

"*Crime Patrol*," Ananya joked.

"You are not even serious."

"I am not, and now can we change the topic?" The conversation ended there.

Amanda was not a person who would give up easily. She made it a point to call on Ananya's mom when she travelled to London on business and 'spilled the beans' about the whole Vicky episode.

"Dear, you are still very young . . ." Ananya's mom wasted no time calling her that weekend and took it from there. "You have your whole life ahead of you, *beta*!"

"I do not understand . . . what . . . you are saying?"

"Don't say no immediately to Vicky."

"Oh that? Who told you?" Ananya was beside herself.

"Amanda was here, *beta*."

"In London? Oh God! She reached London with the news? Oh God, this girl!"

"She had come here on official work."

"That's great backbiting, ha? Ma, it is nothing like you are thinking. She has just blown it out of proportion."

"Still, give it a chance, go out, something could work out?" Her mom was utterly persuasive. "*Beta,* listen, I will not be alive for the rest of your life. If something works out, then nothing is wrong with that, *na*? What is wrong, *beta*, in going out for a cup of coffee?" She went on, "It's only coffee?"

"No, I am not, Ma, you do not understand! I cannot go out with anyone, even if it is Vicky! I still love Rahul!"

"Loving Rahul is not a taboo, but being unfair to yourself is."

"Oh God, Ma? How is your health?" Ananya changed the topic. "When are you visiting me?" The conversation ended that weekend with Ananya changing the topic again.

#

One weekend, Ananya woke up to find the paper *Mumbai News* reporting about the drug pedlars in the city. She blinked at the headline as she collected milk and the morning papers from her doorstep. Her eyes feasted on the pictures of masked criminals in police custody on the first page itself! They were being tried in the city's fast-track court for instant justice. The whole paper of that day ran interesting stories on drug pedlars operating from abandoned locations in the city.

She recognised the picture of the building under construction that she had clicked with her SLR. There were several articles on the rules to be followed for construction of new buildings to avoid mishaps in the future. The head line was Stringent Rules Are Laid Down by the Authorities for Fresh Constructions in the City. Another headline was New Concrete Structures in the City Come under Scanner. She fell back and closed her eyes. *Mumbai News* was, after all, not the most popular 'News Scavenger' for nothing. It was fast and furious! Within a month of her reporting, the criminals were brought to book! Ananya smiled at the thought of Editor Allen D'Cruz. Irrespective of her initial impression, she became a fan of the paper.

A feeling of utter satisfaction that can only come to someone dedicated to great service came to her. She felt indirectly responsible for bringing justice to the parents struggling with drug-addicted teenagers in the city. Ananya thanked her career. After all, she could serve the society in so many ways that no one could think of! The stories were so interesting that she did not get up from the sofa till she had read every word, as Marriamma poured another and yet another cup of hot morning tea for her!

Vicky poured another peg of A&W Root Beer for himself and his father.

From the king suite, they watched the fountains of Bellagio. The dynamic show was all about romancing the senses. The show of water, music, and light thoughtfully interwoven against the lavender sky of Las Vegas was made to mesmerise its admirers. It was a choreographically complex water feature found only at Bellagio.

"I am going to make the Mumbai Palace Villa better than this, Pa! You will see. It will become the hub of international travellers."

His father nodded.

His parents had come into his room for the second evening for quality time.

When in Vegas, he loved living in 'The Bellagio', as it offered luxury in abundance. The rooms, gourmet restaurants, great shopping experience, and romance along with a healthy dose of cultural entertainment. The package was perfectly suited to the wealthy Aroras. This was his parents forty-sixth trip to Vegas in two years. Vicky had joined them for 'together time' after a business meeting in Los Angles.

They had two king-sized suites booked for a week— One for Vicky and the other for his parents. His mom was busy going through the brochures of Bellagio that offered a lot of shopping and busied herself changing the channels on the flat HD TV.

"This fountain show is really miraculous. Every time I see it, I want to see it again." She added aloud, "This is the place for the honeymooners and lovers." She winked, looking at Vicky!

After witnessing the fountain show, Vicky ordered a baked squash with a salad of radicchio, walnuts, and Parmesan for himself. His parents shared a roasted California fennel with olive tapenade, feta, and mint paprika and red pepper soup with pistachio puree between them.

His mom joked, "It's a honeymoon destination, so sharing of food is mandatory." While the truth was they had only vegetarian light meals in the night.

Vicky nodded.

"We will hopefully come with your wife in the near future." His mom persisted. "Find someone fast, or I have a list ready," she added with a smile.

Vicky just sat quietly.

At around 1.30 in the night, the senior Aroras retired to their suite.

Vicky switched off the lights and slid under the satiny sheets, watching the strip from the long full-length glass windows.

"Please consider coming out for another cup of coffee," he had requested Ananya. She was leaving their home in Mumbai that Friday. "I really get to learn a lot in your company."

The truth was she made him happy. Her very presence was enough to light up a room, bring that spark into everything.

"I do not have that kind of time really, sir," she had said, putting a distance between them immediately. "I needed to come today to give the cheque! Thank you once more for everything!" she had added in a sweep.

"The pleasure was mine! I understand!" They were walking to her car, which was parked in his portico.

"I don't know what your parents should think of me? Your mom is so classy. I must have cut a poor figure in front of her in these drab clothes."

He had just moved his head in disagreement.

How could he tell her that he was tired of the classy high-society women? He had started to love the natural free demeanour of Ananya, which was so refreshingly new and different to him!

"'Illustrious' is the word for your parents! That is the right word to describe your parents!"

"You have words for everything, don't you?" Vicky responded, amused.

"Yes, like I have a word called 'centred' for you!"

"Oh, really . . . 'centred'? What does that mean?"

"Never mind." They had reached her car by now. He opened the door on the driver's side.

"Thanks a lot once again for coming."

"Thanks," she said, and without looking back and without another word, she drove off into the night.

He turned restlessly on the bed; it was three in the morning. The strip had become livelier; his lids were heavily closing. His heart was falling too for a woman called Ananya. He sighed. He looked out drowsily; somehow the famous strip did not excite him this time as much as it had on his previous visits. He closed his eyes. He had a feeling of flying into the clouds, so as he fell into a deep dreamless sleep.

#

Vicky was flying back home first-class Emirates. He closed the sliding door to his suite and poured himself a goblet of white wine from the inbuilt minibar and adjusted the ambient lighting to read. His parents had occupied the suites next to his. His life was anything but a haven of luxury. He pursued his dreams big time. He was extremely content on that front. He had turned twenty-eight that February and was the most eligible bachelor in town. Very few knew that he was bored and detested the hollow, artificial women around him. So he did not date any of the girls in his circles, nor did he plan to do so. He looked for genuine honesty in a woman with an identity of her own. He had a book in his hands, but his mind was with Ananya.

'I don't know what to expect from her or what the future will hold for me with her? How things would work out? I only know that I love her company and we have something between us that I cannot lay a finger to. She is always herself. There lies the magic to Ananya Bhatt. I am dying to know more about this woman.' The very thought of her made him happy.

#

Ananya was not dying to know anything! She too felt the magic! Only, she was not ready to lay a finger on it and work on the friendship that was naturally there! A gifted woman's intuition rang alarm bells, warned her to stay away, to avoid him carefully, and not to look at something that was so naturally beautiful between them. Maybe she did not want to get hurt one more time, get bruised one more time! Naturally, Ananya carefully avoided Vicky!

'There is no reason why someone should not like him. Right now, my priority is my baby and work,' she told herself firmly.

Ananya's life changed fast! Now that her publication was doing well, she was hounded continuously by tempting offers with hefty pay packages at least three times more than *AFTER TEA* from some of the best in the industry.

"If you do not take the offers now, you may never get them later. It is one of the fastest growing industry, dear," Amanda warned Ananya. "Most people work in small or medium publishing houses for just six months or so to get into bigger ones. It's a hot seat baby! There are hundreds ready to eat up your position! Don't forget that!"

In the same breath, Amanda asked, "Hey . . . how is Vicky by the way?"

Ananya avoided the question by steering the conversation elsewhere.

#

Ananya felt a little insecure after Amanda's advice. There was much truth in what her friend was saying! She was self-made and not a trained journalist like the youngsters were! If she did not take up the offers, she might wither in a fast-moving industry! Besides, *AFTER TEA* was her baby! She had resurrected it from nothing and slaved on to pump life into it! Now that it was enjoying the outcome of her relentless efforts, was it time to move on? The thought of breaking away from it was too painful. Her small team was her family! Working apart from them also was unthinkable! Ananya had learnt in the year she worked with *AFTER TEA* that professional decisions could not be taken emotionally! Being in the same place might stunt her learning, or it might be seen as incompetence by outsiders! Besides, she did not want to jump to any publication, though it seemed promising. Now at this juncture in life, she was looking for stability, and that could only come from a very established publication. She had to consider a lot of other factors apart from her genre of work to grow professionally. She needed to diversify, learn, and experiment too! There were only two options left for her—either she stuck on and stagnated, or took a risk and jumped on to a new offer to grow professionally. It was one of the most difficult decisions of her life! She had to take it fast!

#

One of those days, Sharbani Goswami called again.

"You took up editing *Starbust*? Congrats!" Amanda screamed over the phone on knowing about it. "Good decision . . . it's the best film magazine in town, I think. People will commit suicide to get an opportunity to work with magazines like that."

"They offered five times more salary, dear. Besides, it is 100 years old!" Ananya rejoined, even as her heart cried for leaving *AFTER TEA*.

That was not the whole reason, why she skipped jobs! In the heart of hearts, Ananya was uncomfortable with the developments of her friendship with Vicky. They had become friends too fast! They got along too well! They shared a lot of likes and dislikes, including their passion for food, historical monuments, and writing! To top it all, he was regally handsome and rich! Besides, her best friend Amanda and her mom added 'fuel to fire'! All Ananya wanted to do was run and she did to a fabulous opportunity that presented itself!

Book IV

WINTER

Every opportunity her family got they touched upon the most interesting topic 'Vicky' to Ananya's trepidation!

In the meanwhile, Ananya's mom roped in her brother. He started to advise her too.

"Please, dear! You do not get good guys every day . . . like Vicky!"

"Bro? How do you know that he is good? . . . It's the pots of money which is visible to people."

"I recommend the pots then! I only see them! Lots!" her brother joked, "You need not work for the rest of your life!"

"Who told you I don't want to?"

"My little sister, darling, go out with him."

"Even if I do, how do you know that I will end up with him?"

"Exactly! Please give it an honest thought, go out and find out."

"He just asked me once, and you guys have no business but to marry me off to him? what a joke! How are the children?" Ananya changed the topic.

#

The new place gave Ananya a lot of time to think over her life. Apart from the regular routine, her life was boring. Besides, her mom was extremely persistent. She called now many times and made sure to touch upon the subject 'VICKY'. Ananya had her mom's words by heart.

"**Beta, time will pass by you. One day you will repent about your decision. It is in your hands. Our times were different! We had a lot of support system. Alia will need a father figure soon. All children do! Consider the little one if not yourself.**"

Ananya always mostly ended the conversation with "Yes, Mom, you guys only want to tie me down with some pretext."

#

'On some pretext or the other the starlets are taken for a ride. The bottom line is that casting couch exists in Bollywood.' Ananya was editing a story on casting couch sitting in her glass cabin at the *Starbust* office, Nariman Point. She edited the next lines: 'Casting couch involves different kinds of sexual favours, from kissing to heavy petting, given and demanded by people for a professional favour in the entertainment industry.' She changed a few atrocious cuss words here and there, tongue-in-cheek. She checked the lines now. They looked perfect. In between, she adjusted the photo frame on her huge table.

It was the same picture that she had on the table of **AFTER TEA** office. It was a picture of the three of them—Rahul, she, and Alia from San Diego zoo; the difference was the venue, table, and cabin. She looked up to see one of her team members, a peppy subeditor, walking past her door. Ananya smiled as their eyes met.

The girl, a feisty twenty-something, saluted her and smiled as she passed. This was how most of her team greeted her non-verbally, from a distance, saluting her or just nodding.

She looked back at the copy. She edited more cuss words, moving her head in disapproval.

"It's your background, dear," Sharbani would often say to her. "You are not used to this language, because you are from a lifestyle magazine! But surely you will, with time!"

"NEVER," Ananya would rejoin. "I will try always to maintain the basic decency and decorum while composing the copy. After all, starlets are humans too."

"Suit yourself," Sharbani would say. "As long as it sells, I have no problems." Sharbani was promoted to senior vice-president's position, and Ananya had taken her place as the chief editor of *Starbust*.

Ananya sighed. Her team at *Starbust* was huge in numbers and qualifications. They were a bunch of professionals and rascals who were ready to do anything to get a story. She was amongst the best and the worst in a way; most vigorous in the market and ready to kill, her team did not operate by moral values or ethics when it came to work. She needed special skills to handle them at their level to bring them to hers. She could not say how they felt about her, but after a month into *Starbust*, she was getting used to them.

'A starlet has sued a famous producer' she edited the line finally.

She edited the next part of the sentence 'for asking her for unnatural sex.' After deleting the cuss words, the edited sentence read,

'A starlet has sued a famous producer for asking her for unnatural sex.'

In the new office, the copies that she edited were much, much different from what she was used to at ***AFTER TEA***. It was never hands-on as the stories came to her almost complete. Ananya just had to scan them for mistakes. She wanted to make *Starbust* a classy film magazine, contrary to the raunchy image it had! Word had spread around in the new place, about her, as a competent, able professional, but the bottom line was 'Ananya was a small-time editor for a huge set-up like *Starbust*'. She knew that she had a big responsibility and a wayward, headstrong team on her hands! It was a learning of a different kind, and she was loving the challenge!

#

"I know that you have to take urgent meetings, work at a larger level, edit a 100 times more harder, but also I know that you are avoiding me like flu."

"I know that you are not flu, so?" She had a gentle flutter in her tummy and her heart had started to race at his voice!

It was Vicky. He had called from an unknown number.

"Why are you avoiding me then?"

"I quit ***AFTER TEA*** . . . soo . . . so got busy. I am not avoiding anyone," she said, carefully emphasising on the latter.

"I found your mail resignation letter. It was sudden. I wanted to ask you in person."

"All things in life are sudden," Ananya quoted Mr Swaminarain from All India Journalists' Association.

"You have become a philosopher, eh? I did not want to stop you and create a misunderstanding like you already have."

Ananya's heart missed a beat; in spite of herself, she felt elated at this rejoinder.

"Misunderstanding? I was, eer . . ." She could not find words to continue.

"Don't you think that we talk well and jell well?" he asked.

She remained silent.

"So why are you avoiding me?"

"Who said I am . . . I am plain busy."

"Give me a break. I am also busy, but I am not avoiding you. How is Alia?"

She avoided the first rejoinder and responded to the next. "Alia is just great and growing up fine."

"Can you show a little courtesy, by the way?"

"As in?"

"As in, meet me in person and explain about you leaving *AFTER TEA* all of a sudden? 'Running' from it is the right word, or you don't want to now?"

How could she tell him about her fears?

"Ah, errr, can I call back? I am in the middle of something, so . . . besides, it was just a professional decision, nothing personal!" She bit her tongue.

"Oh, was it? You seem busier than the president of this country, and you will take months to call back, madam," he joked.

She felt strangely happy at this rejoinder too, and the prospect of meeting him brought back the 'excitement flutter' back into her stomach. There was a long uncomfortable silence before he spoke again!

"Are you there?"

"Yes!"

"I have a feeling that you were finding reasons to shun me." He was irritating her now.

"No, I am not."

"Prove me wrong!"

"Don't you feel that we are arguing like children?" Ananya's voice rose.

"That's the best part. We bring out the child in each other," he laughed.

In spite of herself, she laughed too. How she missed these conversations!

"Today is Monday. Is this Friday good for you at four?"

She wanted to say no, but said yes. "Can we meet at five?" She just wanted to meet him and finish it.

"My place? Or somewhere else? My parents will be, by the way, very happy to see you." There was excitement in his voice now. "They are already heartbroken about your resignation . . . my father specially."

"Oh, so sweet!" she laughed. "Your place, then. I would love to meet them. That would be really great," Ananya agreed.

After she hung up, Ananya felt happy about Vicky's call.

'Must be all the pressure my folks putting on me. There is no such thing as missing him,' she thought, brushing away the excitement she felt at the very prospect of seeing him again.

"You need to first soak the bitter gourd in curds to kill the bitterness, then squeeze all the water, then fry."

Ananya was discussing a recipe with Mrs Kunika Arora, mother of Vicky Arora.

"Oh, I did not know that! Maybe that is the reason why the bitter gourd is so bitter every time I fry it. My husband loves it, and I often end up making it bitter."

"That is why it is called as the 'bitter gourd'," Ananya added, and both laughed.

The next fifteen minutes, Ananya was busy discussing recipes, social work, methods to eradicate child labour with Mrs Arora, and in the same breath went on to discuss scams in the city and politics with Mr Arora. This was the second visit of hers to Vicky's residence. His parents were already floored by her.

'She has something for everyone.' Vicky marvelled at Ananya's communication skills.

One Friday led to another and another and another. Ananya got along well with the senior Aroras. In fact, they were inseparable. Vicky fell for Ananya more and more as days went by; he knew he had to take the first step. Only, he did not know when and how.

"Please, you must come next Friday," Vicky's mom requested Ananya, when she was leaving. "In fact, you should have never left our job."

Mr Arora nodded, taking slow sips of his cigar.

"Oh, I will try. It's my honour actually that you people love my company," Ananya rejoined in her smooth style as Vicky moved his head incredulously from the corner of the table in the garden, where they were having their evening snacks.

"You are like my parents," Ananya said.

"You must be having your in-laws?" Mrs Arora asked.

Ananya was quiet. Ananya had lost her mother-in-law to cancer within a year of marriage and her father-in-law to a heart attack a year later.

"Hope we are not intruding on something," Mrs Arora said, looking at Ananya's change of expression.

"My parents-in-law are no more."

Both of them gasped. "Oh, we are sorry," said Mrs Arora without further probe.

"Think of us as your family, and after work, drop in here for coffee any time," Mr Arora invited Ananya again.

"I will. I will keep in mind."

"If in case you cannot make it, call me," Vicky joked from his corner . . . "I will take them out. They get bored on weekends without you now."

"As I said, being liked by you people is in true sense pleasurable," she said seriously now. "I will be there whenever I can." She liked to give Mrs Arora company as she was diabetic and loved people around her.

"Can I come over to visit Alia one Saturday when you are home?" Vicky invited himself to Ananya's place when she was leaving his home one Friday.

"Of course you can," she said hesitatingly. Vicky could sense her discomfort and responded quickly!

"If you are uncomfortable then . . ."

"It's not that. I am worried more about your comfort actually."

"My comfort? What happened to that? I was brought up in a humble neighbourhood as a child."

Ananya's eyebrows rose!

"I would love to know more about your childhood then!"

"Some other time. Then coming Saturday?" he asked, persisting.

"No problemo," she laughed. "Five o'clock?"

"No problemo," he rejoined, copying her.

#

"All problems are because of the new editor," Raj, the fiery twenty-something subeditor of *Startbust* story columnist was complaining . . . "See, tomorrow this copy has to go in print and why the hell this lady wants to change it?"

"Did she change the interview?" asked John, another subeditor of Trivia column from the adjacent cubicle.

"No, my spirit of writing is lost because of all the editing of those glamorous . . . cuss . . ." his voice trailed, without completing the sentence.

John laughed along with Nikita, another colleague and subeditor from glamour division.

"I think you should ask her," Nikita advised, "instead of backbiting. I think she is in her cabin. Go right now."

"I will F#^&@% will."

John and Nikita were in peals at the expense of Raj.

Ananya checked the watch; it was 12 noon.

'Still time for lunch,' thought she, but she could feel pre-meal hunger pangs. 'I will fetch a drink now that the editing is over.'

When she was about to get up, her desk phone rang.

"Ananya Bhatt, chief editor *Starbust*."

'Sure you are,' thought Raj . . . instead, he asked, "Ma'am, I want to see you. I am Subeditor Raj."

"Raj? Come right in," Ananya said without further words.

Raj was sitting in front of Ananya without a word for ten minutes now, observing her. She was new to him as he was to her.

Ananya spoke slowly, measuring her words . . . "I love the spirit of your writing, Raj. There is no doubt about it. So will the readers. The story is fresh and fabulous with a new angle to it."

Raj observed Ananya's razor-sharp nose and her beautiful eyes . . . he was floored . . .

'She is beautiful. Fu#$%@^ beautiful,' he thought. 'But that does not mean she is good!'

Ananya was saying, "There is no doubt that you have done a marvellous job, dear, but don't you feel we need to give due respect to women? Whether she is a starlet or a prostitute? At least in our writings?" Ananya added.

Raj's mind flew to his long-term girlfriend who had left him a week before.

"You have no respect for me," she had wailed. "I am always taken for granted," she had howled . . . "Using me and abusing me," she had cried like a child. The truth was, he was missing his girlfriend now and had no clue going about amending his relationship with her. "You bastard! May you rot in hell!" she had screamed before leaving him.

Ananya's words brought him back to reality. "If you think your original copy was good, which it was, we will carry it. Besides, if you think that by just removing some words, it has become ineffective, we will keep the original!"

Raj simply stood up. "I think I understand your point, ma'am. Let's include the 'no cuss words' story," he said, stressing on the latter part.

Ananya nodded. "OK then! I am proud to have you in my team, Mr Raj. You have amazing writing skills."

Raj felt great. He was surprised at Ananya's amicable, down-to-earth attitude. Most senior editors like her would give a damn about the stories of junior teammates like him. The stories written by them were never even considered. That was the reason he was so defensive before meeting her! 'She will be around for a long time to come,' he thought. Upon reaching the door, he looked back. "Ma'am?"

Ananya looked up from her machine. "Welcome to *Starbust.*"

"Thanks," Ananya reciprocated with a twinkle in her eye, adding, "Now the copy needs to be sent for print tomorrow. It is that F$#@^&* Saturday!" He could not suppress a laugh. Ananya laughed with him.

#

One Saturday led to another. From the first day itself, Alia took to Vicky.

Vicky found Ananya's home very cosy, and he loved the close-knit neighbourhood. It reminded him of his childhood. He must have been three when they shifted to a nearby small apartment for a decade, when his father was embroiled in a legal battle over the ancestral home with his uncles.

"This home reminds me of my childhood apartment."

"Oh, really? I am happy about that, but I thought your home is big?"

"I know, I know. It's a long story!"

"I would love to hear it."

"Some other day!"

Alia and Vicky got along like a house on fire! The times he was in Ananya's home he was on the floor, building structures, making dinosaurs with clay, making animal sounds, romping around, and making noise. Alia clapped and screamed non-stop. When Vicky stopped, she threw a tantrum for more. He was forced to comply.

"You asked for it," Ananya laughed one Saturday when he was visiting them.

"I enjoy playing with her. She seems to have more stamina than me," Vicky laughed. "Really!"

Alia got Vicky to make the buildings again that day.

This time, he was building a hotel with the blocks. "See, see, look, look, Alia, look this is a hotel."

Alia repeated, "HOOOOOttteeeee," clapping.

Ananya wanted to laugh . . . 'He is building a hotel here too.' Instead, she smiled at the thought.

Alia looked with open wonder and again blabbered something, clapping.

"Look now, I am putting the last block and . . . and . . . and . . . and . . ." The structure moved a bit, and Alia started to clap in anticipation, moving from side to side.

The blocks fell, and she was in peals of laughter again.

Ananya watched them, revelling in the most beautiful moments of her life . . . Later, as she tucked tiny Alia into bed that night and lay next to her, her mother's words came to her. She reflected on the pure immeasurable pleasures of having a family. She only knew how much she missed it! She remembered Rahul, and her eyes brimmed in months.

Without her own volition, Ananya started to look forward to Vicky's visits.

#

The next time Vicky came visiting, Ananya's mom and brother took turns speaking to him over the phone. They were ecstatic and gushed later about what a nice person he was and how different he sounded!

In actuality, Ananya knew that Vicky was like a prince for her simple, middle-class folks. They, in their wildest dreams, could have never imagined interacting with a famous, filthily rich, suave man like him. Ananya simply pitied them! Little Alia too had taken to him! Fate had thrown Vicky at her in the most unexpected of ways!

Not only that, Ananya felt hopeless as the life she had so carefully created threatened to slip away from her hands. Her little world threatened to rock! Her mind and heart were in constant battle. Sometimes her heart won and sometimes her mind. Sometimes the mother in her wanted a family for Alia, and at other times she decided that she was better off without a man. Even if he was someone like Vicky!

As the days passed, she buried herself in work and concentrated on Alia, shutting Vicky, out of her life! She chose to close the unexpected, unnerving chapter forever and ever. She assured herself that the new office and demands on her time would bring normalcy and peace back into life with her little one! As her work gave her satisfaction, her decision brought her unexpected pain!

#

During the three months that they spent with each other's families, Vicky's parents knew that something serious was brewing as they did not miss the growing 'lost look' on their son's face. On the other hand, Vicky could sense a change in Ananya's demeanour. Lately, she had distanced herself from him, in a seeming effort to brace away from him. Understanding her situation perfectly, he maintained a stoic silence himself, which only increased his longing and pain for her.

"Do you like Ananya?" asked his mom one day gingerly as they were relaxing together in the lawns after dinner.

Vicky nodded.

"I don't mind having her as my . . . !" He looked at her sharply! She smiled sweetly, nodding.

"Will I be perfect for her? Will she be perfect for me?"

"There are no perfect people, dear. There can be perfect relationships, though. We need to work towards them."

That was the moment when he decided.

'God, please do not allow the bustier to give way, God . . . please! I am not so used to this,' Ananya prayed.

'I am plain nervous for nothing,' she told herself the next moment.

She had pulled the gown over her body, tugging it a little higher than required over her bosom.

'We can assume it wasn't Anne Hathaway's goal to be upstaged by her own nipples.' Ananya had read that somewhere . . . while doing a story on the actress's red carpet appearance for the Oscars that year.

'Hope I am not upstaging mine . . . today!'

She tugged at the dress for adjustments, checking and rechecking it from all angles, while the script played in her mind.

'I thank my friends.'

She adjusted the dress over the waist, armpits, bosom. 'As they say, beneath the glamour is where the things really get interesting at the Oscars . . . power bleach, armpit Botox, cleavage facials.

'I had none of it. I don't require it. I am not an actress,' she told herself . . . . 'Now zip it!' She zipped her gown. 'My words are more important, not my boobs!'

'I thank my friends, ummm, umm, *haan* colleagues, no . . . no, it's the friends, then, . . . colleagues.' She applied lipstick, a sheer stick of delicate red from Elizabeth Arden.

'Then family . . . then, mmmm . . . family, yes, yes, family.'

'Ma?' she shouted. 'After the family comes . . . now repeat . . .' she told herself . . . 'colleagues, friends . . . oh God, I forgot . . . again, no, no, last comes the family!'

She finished with the lipstick and dabbed it with a tissue and reapplied a fresh coat.

"Ma! Are you ready?"

"Yes, almost!" Her mom shouted back from the next room.

She checked herself one last time in the full-length mirror in her room.

The gown hugged her lean body at the waist, tapering down full length to the ground; the silk encased in delicate net hugged her bosom, while the extra one inch over the bustier gave away her rich skin underneath, yet camouflaging dramatically the beginning of the curves, which she did not want to show. Her thick black-brown hair was swept back in a neat Victorian-style bun at the nape; her neat silver clutch and delicate jewellery were in harmony with the delicate diamond clips in her hair and manicured fingers.

She slid into her smooth silver Jimmy sandals that fit to perfection and applied black Elizabeth Arden kohl and double-density mascara, working on the lashes with a safety pin to remove the tangles. She had read somewhere about foot lipo for Oscars and laughed to herself. 'I don't care about my feet really. I think I can do better with anti-anxiety drugs, instead, which the Hollywood actors take.' She took the clutch and walked out of her room with one final look at herself.

"Ma?"

Her mom came out from the adjacent room with sleeping Alia on her shoulder; She was in a 'blue-purple' *Kancheepuram* checks sari with a neat Indian-type bun.

"I think the *pallu* is very long." She adjusted the *pallu* with one hand, balancing Alia with the other. From the moment her mom landed, Alia was inseparable from her.

"Ma, it's perfect. You look like Bhanu Rekha."

"Really?" Rekha was her mom's favourite yesteryears Bollywood actress, the ultimate style diva.

"Really, Ma!"

In return, her mom pulled and adjusted Ananya's gown over her bosom a little higher. "You should have also worn sari, *na*?"

Ananya smiled, moving her head.

"Ma, don't pull it up further, or it will give way . . ."

Marriamma took Alia from her grandma's hands.

"Feed her well the boiled *khichadi* that I taught you yesterday, *haan*?" Her mom told Marriamma the hundredth time. "Before eight o'clock . . . no, no, between seven and eight."

Marriamma nodded, smiling, and Ananya made an apologetic face at her.

Ananya's mom bent and gave a peck on the sleeping Alia's cheek. "They look like angels when they are sleeping, *na*?" she exclaimed.

"Yes, Ma! Hurry, we need to go all the way to Taj!"

The Taj Mahal hotel overlooking the Arabian Sea was a magnificent monumental construction, at least 100 years old. It was also the place for most of the high-profile parties and award functions. Who's who from the publishing industry, Bollywood, and the fashion industry were expected that day. It was a national event of the most extraordinary type! It was the 'Oscars' of the print media.

Five o'clock, 8 February 2013—Ananya was comfortably seated in her Mahindra SUV XUV 500 that she had recently bought. It was a chauffeur-driven luxury in flamboyant red.

'It's been a long journey of 100 years in one whole year,' she thought as the vehicle moved ahead.

She looked at her mom. She was humming an old Bollywood number under her breath . . . the diamond studs shone in the afternoon sun. She caught Ananya looking at her and smiled sweetly, her nose stud glistening!

"What, *beta*?"

"Ma, thank you for coming."

"I had to. I want to be a part of your life, *na*? Your happiness and your pain! God forbid . . ." Her voice trailed emotionally. With a gentle hand she tried to adjust Ananya's dress again.

Ananya just caught her hand and put it to her cheek. "I love you, Ma, for everything. Love you. I missed you so much!"

Her mom only smiled and looked away at the traffic, misty-eyed.

"Ma, why don't you just rest? Sleep for a while . . . It's a long way to the Taj Hotel . . . you must be jet-lagged?"

"I will." Her mom sniffed into her handkerchief.

The SUV took a turn to the Western Expressway, they came to the Times of India signal. A small boy came running with a bunch of blood-red roses. He was making faces at her to buy them. She just smiled and moved her hand for him to go away. He did not.

The memory of another evening at the same signal, buying roses from a small street boy came to her. She blushed.

The evening cast long shadows. Her SUV zoomed ahead. Her mind relieved the past months like a story postcard. Her life had taken an unexpected turn.

#

She was in the middle of a cover photo shoot for *Starbust* a couple of months back when it all happened.

One-film-old Minky Das had already developed starry airs. She landed an hour late at the studios; she laid down the condition that she did not want television channels to cover the shoot. (Generally, there was a tie-up between *Starbust* photo shoots and some Bollywood promo channels, which Ananya had to cancel at the last moment.) To top it, Minky's boyfriend landed there, making things worse. When Ananya reached the studios that afternoon to check personally, Minky was locked up inside the make-up room with him, while the make-up artist was cooling his heels outside. Ananya could not cancel the shoot as her subeditor had already done the main story on the actress and the copy was ready for print! Ananya had no choice but to carry on! Minky was very co-operative during the interview earlier but went into a different mode altogether for the shoot.

Ananya knocked on the make-up room; her boyfriend opened the door to reveal a half-naked Minky sleeping on the dresser and smoking weed. She came out after much persuasion from Ananya to carry on with the make-up.

"All *nakhra*s, madam . . ." The hairstylist made a dirty disgusted face as Ananya came out of the make-up room after convincing Minky.

"*Abhi woh* hairstyle *me bhi problem karegi . . .*" (Now she will create problems for the hairstyles), the hairstylist said, moving her head in disapproval.

It was not all. Later, Minky, moved around wearing next-to-nothing in the studios. She did not approve of the dress selected by *Starbust*; she wanted to expose and create a sensation—the demands were endless! Finally, she approved of a backless sheer white short dress above her thighs. Once in the dress, she wanted to pose with her underpants exposed. Ananya made her understand the theme of the cover story; when nothing worked, her publicist secretary was roped in. After hours of delay, Minky posed for pictures, and the shoot progressed. In all this commotion, Ananya's phone started ringing. She ignored the calls many a times, but as the caller seemed to be persistent, she had no choice but to come out of the studio to take it.

"Hello?"

"Today is Friday, and it's almost two months that we have met," said a familiar voice. It was Vicky.

'Oh God! It had to be him now of all people!' Her stomach convulsed. Even in the midst of a commotion, she felt happy at the very sound of his voice. She kicked herself for that.

"You always call from unknown numbers and surprise me."

"I have so many phones, I should utilise them," he joked. "Besides, I don't want you to avoid me."

"How do you know I am?"

"Because you never call. It's me who does."

"Not so, well read . . ." Ananya lied.

"I wanted to see you today." He came to the point straight like always.

"Ah, I am in the middle of . . . it's not possible really. Besides . . . I wanted to . . ."

"Maintain a distance. Finding ways to dissuade meeting me?"

"Will you stop thinking for me? Stop over-reading, stop imitating, and stop whatever . . . I don't have the time. Besides . . . I wanted to go home after this . . ." Ananya added, exasperated more at herself for overreacting.

At that point, the production fellow came out in search of her.

"Look, I need to go in now. I came out of the studio for this call!"

"Please come and see me today . . . I will never ask you again . . ." he cajoled. "Where are you right now?"

"Opposite to the fountain in a studio actually." She did not want to disclose her location. She had no control over things as he always had his way, and she seemed to comply.

"So, you are not very far from my office, eh? Give me the address and I will come, pick you."

"You don't give up easily, do you?" The production guy was signalling frantically from the door by now!

"Nope!"

The production guy almost looked, as if he will cry!

She gave the address.

The shoot was over in an hour, and Vicky came to pick her up.

"I have only an hour. I need to rush back home," she said taking the seat next to him in his black BMW.

"I heard that ten times now at least. I will not take long either. Fasten your seat belt!"

She did.

"Where are we going?" He did not reply.

Instead he asked, "How is Alia?"

"She is good."

"I miss her."

She did not say anything.

Surprise of surprises, she was relieved to see him. She was, in fact, happy sitting next to him again. It hit her suddenly, that she missed him too.

She repeated, "Where are we going?"

"Don't worry, I am not taking you to a battlefield."

'He must be driving us home. Anyways, with him around, I am in constant battle with myself! It does not make a difference where he takes me!' She thought wryly, unable to fight herself!

She observed him from the corner of her eye as he drove . . . He was wearing a pair of casual jeans and a navy blue Calvin Klein T-shirt that accentuated his perfectly shaven face. She could not but wonder how rustically Aryan he looked, and every time she met him, she could not mistake that pull she felt for him.

He drove them to the Gateway of India.

"Want to get out for a walk?" he asked, once he had parked the car at the cobbled pathway to the gate.

She nodded. He never failed to surprise her.

They walked slowly towards the arch.

"You brought me here to show the Gateway of India?" Ananya asked, amused.

They were standing at the centre of the arch, eighty-three feet above ground level, after some time . . .

"You like historical places, so I thought . . ."

"So I do not always go looking for them after a hard day's work."

He suddenly said, "How amazing it is . . . look up."

She did.

When she looked down, he was on one knee with a ring in his hand. She was speechless.

"What?"

Vicky was saying, "Ms Ananya Bhatt! You are the most magical woman to happen to me! You will continue to interest and intrigue me for the rest of my life. Will you be mine forever?"

Her eyes popped out. Words just froze in her throat; seconds seemed like eternity; the background sounds vanished . . . the sound of the waves, the squawking of the seagulls, everything dimmed. The ancient sculpted dome above her started to go in circles till she thought she would faint . . . she froze on the spot for how long she could not tell. A couple of foreign tourists watched them amusedly as they moved about.

Finally, after what seemed to be an eternity, she found her voice . . . "All, all of . . . of . . . of a sudden? Just like that? I was not expecting . . . expecting all this now. Why? I mean you . . . you?"

"You will expect this some time, isn't it if I ask you out on dates? I also know for sure that you would have found ways to dissuade me if I did . . . so why waste time? When I know that you are the one?"

She had started to shiver at the sudden unexpected turn of events . . . A small group of child vendors and urchins gathered to watch them, showing fingers at them and making faces. As it was a working day, thankfully, except for a few foreign tourists, there was no crowd.

"What are you thinking? I am still on my knees, Ananya?" Ananya's hair waved in the sea breeze as she blushed a crimson red.

"I don't think . . . that . . . I am worth . . ." Her voice trembled.

"What? That you are not young, beautiful, charming, and sexy? Or if I can get a girl with all these qualities . . . why you?"

She said, trembling, "I have a pa . . . pas . . ." She could not just go on.

"You have a past that still hangs on you?"

She nodded, furious . . . that he could again snatch the words from her.

"But you are everything I want in a woman . . . I just know it . . . In fact, I had fallen for you the moment you walked into my office the very first day . . . with a stained white shirt and a messy confused expression . . . only, only, I discovered it later."

"Oh! Oh! My shirt, it was . . . it was Alia," Ananya stammered unable to talk. "Why did you hire me then?" she said, suddenly angry.

"I wanted to give you a chance," he laughed "Actually it was your speech that did the trick."

"Speech?"

"Yes! The fiery speech . . . of goldmine thing?"

"Oh, goldmine? I don't remember."

"You don't, but I do . . . I want you to give me a chance now!" he added.

The street children were around them, watching amusedly. They were prompting Ananya in Hindi, "*Haan bol, haan bol . . . ek picture mein dekha tha aisa hi scene*" (Say yes, say yes . . . we have seen the same situation in a Hindi film).

Ananya did not know whether to laugh or to cry standing there.

"We are making a scene," she mumbled. Vicky just laughed without budging.

Ananya's hair blew in the golden red light of the setting sun. Her heart was beating a million times louder and faster. Words were not helping her either. Street urchins were dancing around them now, singing some filmy songs.

She found herself saying at last, "I am, I am not yet over my husband Rahul."

"Call it Bohemian, but it is attractive . . . for me."

"That will remain so after 100 years." She added suddenly, "Rahul was my first love . . . he will remain so."

"That is more attractive," Vicky rejoined on one knee.

"It is not going to be easy for you. I am a mom . . . my little girl is my world . . .".

"I know that already."

The sun cast a crimson red in the background. The shadows were longer now. Vicky was on his knees still. She felt warm tears in her eyes. By now her throat was parched.

"If I say yes to you and if I lose you, I will never be the same again. I will not have the strength to stand up . . . you must understand . . . that"

"I love you. I will never let that happen even in a 100 years . . . ," he said, smiling; it infuriated her more.

"Anything else?"

Her mother's words came to her "I won't be alive forever . . . you need someone . . . 'I want to make sure before anything . . . ,' she thought but said aloud,

"I have discovered something this past year. I can never give up for the rest of my life."

Vicky looked at her quizzically. "What?"

"My work!"

"Thank God! . . . you scared the s&*%#* out of me. OK, done! You can keep it!"

"I have an extremely independent streak in me, and I love earning my bucks."

"Of course!" he mocked. "You can have it all . . . will you marry me now?"

"I am very, very temperamental. I bring work pressures home. Not only that, you will have to fit into my little world in my scheme of things. That will take a lot of effort on your part! That will make you unhappy sometimes!" She felt disappointed at what she was saying. The thought of losing him now was too painful for her. She waited with bated breath.

"Is it necessary to discuss it all here? People are listening," he joked.

"I want to make sure!"

"Then listen! I love the very fact that you are self-made, you work, do not want to give it up for anything in this world. I love your down-to-earth, honest, upfront attitude. I love that you are a mom, you are real, you are that proverbial child-woman. I also know that if I do not propose to you today I will not to anyone for a long, long time. I will never find another YOU!"

A couple of women tourists came up the platform to look at the sculpted dome . . . Seeing the duo, they started clicking pictures . . . The urchins also came and went, curious to see the developments in the proposal . . . Ananya's red-green *kammez* and *dupatta* blew like a windcheater in the strong ocean breeze. The huge tears in her eyes . . . shone like dewdrops.

"I cannot stand and wipe those tears," Vicky joked. "I cannot do it till you respond to me!" He looked around, smiling at the people and winked at the urchins.

The women started clicking more pictures.

Vicky said, "I will accept your child as mine. I will accept the fact that I am not your first love . . . Marry me because I want to give you the best life . . . Marry me because I want to grow old with you."

Ananya just nodded speechlessly. He slid the ring on to her finger. The onlookers cheered and clapped.

"Take your time, darling! We have a whole lifetime!" he said on standing up.

She lifted her eyebrows in mock surprise . . . and the 112-year-old dome echoed their laughter!

#

Ananya jerked back from her thoughts as her vehicle pulled at a traffic signal.

Ananya just smiled at the crowding child vendors at the signal . . . A man with a squint eye was selling mobile chargers. Some children were selling strawberries and colourful feather dusters, while a woman beggar with a sleeping cherubic baby on her arm begged for alms.

"Dear! I really missed all this in UK!" Her mom had opened her eyes a fraction. "I am going to sleep again. God! you will need a bulldozer to wake me, I really am jet-lagged," she said, yawning.

Ananya laughed and said, "I will wake you much before the venue. Don't worry, Ma."

Her mom closed her eyes with a hand on Ananya's arm, and in a short while, she was fast asleep.

The vehicle started to move ahead, and Ananya went back to her thoughts!

#

"One thing I was always dying to know, How did you find out about my baby? You came to the hospital to visit Alia? Remember?" Ananya reminded Vicky in his car later, as they drove back from the Gateway.

"Oh! That? The whole office was agog with the news. Now, I know I did the right thing . . . the magic happened in the hospital too," he smiled moving a gentle finger on her cheek as he put the car into gear.

"Please drop me here," she said as they entered the car parking at the studios.

"It looks deserted. I will wait here till you drive out."

"No worries. The studios are all the same. There must be a shoot happening somewhere."

She was about to get out, when he held her hand in a vice-like grip.

"Please don't go . . ." he said gently.

"I am not leaving you. I am only going home . . . I have a little someone waiting for me back there," she said, her pulse racing at a dangerous speed!

He nodded. "Sooner I get used to it the better, I suppose? I cannot have you at my beck and call."

"You cannot be very typical at least for sure!" she smiled, adding, "You can still think . . ." Her voice trailed immediately as a sense of loss swept over her at her own words, and he loosened his grip. The next moment, without a warning, his head descended to brush her lips gently in a feather-like kiss. He pulled back as fast as he had come close.

"Please do not think that I want to get physical with you now that we are together . . ." His voice was a hoarse whisper.

"Really?" she mocked, trembling on finding her own. She was shivering when she got out of the car a few moments later, and he did the same. In the shadows, under the gulmohar trees, in the quiet nightfall, overcome by emotion, Ananya hugged Vicky. They stayed with their bodies entwined like creepers, till she pulled his head down to passionately claim his lips with hers. In turn, Vicky held Ananya closer, crushing her body against his, while his lips eagerly reciprocated the invitation sought. That moment, the rock on Ananya's finger caught the street light and glistened as she further tightened her grip around his neck!

#

Seven o'clock—her SUV was well on its way and speeding. She looked out of the windows; the traffic was fast on their side of the road. Ananya sighed softly at the memories.

She had a copy of **AFTER TEA** lying on the seat. She affectionately moved her fingers over the meditating monk. It was one of the most outstanding issues of the year. By now they had reached the Queen's Necklace. Ananya could see the gleaming dark waves as the vehicle sped past. The roads glistened on the side in the street lights, complimenting the waves.

She threw a sweet smile to her mom who was awake by now.

"Ma! Get ready to go!"

"How long, baby, now?"

"Maybe another twenty minutes or so?"

"Do you think Alia must be awake now?" Ma asked anxious . . ."Should we call home?"

Ananya said, "No, Ma, Marriamma will, if it is necessary. Don't worry!"

Ananya's mom started dabbing her face with a tissue, adjusted her bun and flowers, and the SUV took a couple of turns. By now they could see the Taj Mahal Hotel.

Ananya said, "This place has a history . . . Ma."

Her mom just looked out and gasped, "It is looking like a palace, *beta*."

"It is actually. For more than a century, the Taj has played a part in the life of this city. It is the place that hosted the maharajas, dignitaries, eminent personalities from across the globe. Today it is hosting this function, Ma," Ananya said emotionally.

As they turned a third time, the historical place came into full view with the Gateway of India in the front.

"Ma? This is the Gateway of India. Vicky proposed to me here," she said showing a finger to the monument.

Her mom craned her neck. "Where?" she asked urgently. "Where, *beta*?"

"There! On the top, in the centre there, look! In the middle of the dome." Her mom simply looked, gaping at it!

Ananya watched the Gateway as the vehicle took a long turn to The Taj. Now they could clearly see the Towering Palace Hotel.

#

Mr Singh, the chief of security, Taj Palace, was given a special guests list that evening with the names of guests, designations, and awards that they won. He was meticulously checking the names on the invitations as the special guests arrived to invite them personally.

He had given special instructions to his staff to look out for a lady called Ananya Bhatt, as Ananya's name topped his list.

Ananya's vehicle neared the Taj; the narrow lane was crammed with people . . . it was also heavily guarded. A security personnel signalled them to stop for checking. He asked for the invitation card. She gave it.

Ananya saw the security guy exchange words with a man in heavy military kind of uniform, obviously his senior. The other security personnel checked the dashboard and the boot of her car. Some instructions were given to them. They took positions on either side of Ananya's car.

"Are they going to fire at us or something?" her mom said in an amused tone . "Imagine coming all the way from London and getting killed here."

"Shhh, Ma," said Ananya nervously.

The senior approached her.

"Ms Ananya?"

She nodded. "That's right."

"I am Mr Singh, the chief of security staff, Taj Palace Hotels . . . we are honoured to invite you to Taj Palace this evening," he said and saluted her. "Welcome, ma'am!"

"You are given a special entrance to the venue," The chief security officer said. "Ma'am, this way!" He stood aside saluting, while the security personnel on either side of the path did the same. Ananya just blinked.

The car passed the VVIP red carpet directly to the entrance where hundreds of journalists, TV crew, and media people were waiting for the celebrities to take interviews, get a glimpse, or to click pictures every time a vehicle approached. There was a clamour and uproar; the security had a tough time keeping them away from the barricaded area.

Ananya's vehicle approached the entrance. There was uproar from hundreds of journalists on either side of the red carpet . . . hundreds of flashbulbs came to life; the crowd went berserk, shouting, asking questions even before she alighted.

"You are a star, *beta*!" her mom said, wiping a tear.

Ananya was in a daze. Her car stopped.

"Ma! Take care of yourself." She stepped out.

Two girl escorts and a boy escort came running towards her.

"Ms Ananya?"

"Yes?"

The escort took position next to her "This way please! Ma'am you can wait to pose for pictures or to give short interviews on way if you want," she informed her.

Ananya saw her mom being escorted by another 'volunteer escort' inside the Taj ballroom. Her mom walked with her chest held high and waved over her shoulder to her as she passed.

The journalists were screaming for a picture. They had no clue which industry she belonged to. There were celebrities from fashion, film, television, and publishing industry that day.

Ananya took slow steps on the red carpet, waving. Hundreds of bulbs flashed.

"Ma'am, this way please. Look here please, ma'am, look here please! Thank you, madam . . . thank you . . . here please . . ."

"Ma'am, are you receiving an award tonight?" A perspiring journalist who almost fell over the barricade gasped.

"Yes . . . I am"

"Ma'am, look here . . . look here, this way, ma'am . . . thank you . . ."

"Which award, ma'am?"

"The best editor . . . National award," said Ananya humbly.

"She is a journalist," he shouted to the journalists standing behind him . . ." WE ARE PROUD OF YOU!" the journalists shouted in a slogan from behind the man. Ananya nodded.

"Madam! Is it your first?" someone asked.

"Yes!" Ananya could only manage a whisper.

#

Amongst the hundreds of journalists was Nandita, waiting over an hour to get a good photograph and an interview for the next day's cover story for her small-time daily. She could not so far picture someone for the cover. The hour just went by clicking at random people; nothing inspirational happened.

It was a big day for Nandita as it was her first outdoor assignment. She desperately wanted to get a good story so that she could fight for a hike. In her late twenties, she was still fighting for a foothold as a journalist. This small daily was her bread and butter with a husband at home with no job, looking after their seven-month-old daughter; she somehow carried on with the hectic life of a photo-journalist, with peanuts for a salary. She never gave up hope. In fact, she dreamt of receiving a national award one day for her work from the president of India!

She wanted her story to have an edge.

The chief editor of her daily was all for skimpily clad starlets. "They increase our popularity and marketability, you know?" He would often tell her, "Get some juicy stories, dear, not the stories of these dry women social workers in cotton saris . . . They are inspirational, but they don't sell."

She saw a red gown pass by with a dazzling smile. She ran after it.

"She is Ms Ananya Bhatt, receiving the Best Editor's National Award," the journalist next to her was saying . . . click . . . click . . . click.

She ran after the gown.

She ran to get the best picture, craning her neck and pushing the crowd. She hit people with her elbows for a better angle. Suddenly, the crowd propelled her, and she was facing Ananya.

"Ma'am! Are you nominated? Are you receiving an award tonight? Which section?"

"I am receiving the award for the **Best Editor at the National level. I am from the lifestyle section.**"

"Now you will become famous! After today!" Nandita screamed above the din truthfully.

"Thanks. It's for ***AFTER TEA***." Nandita had never heard of it before! But there was something about this woman; she liked her instantly.

"Ma'am, I am Nandita from *Free Daily.*"

"Nice meeting you!"

"This is my card . . ." she began, but she got pushed . . . The card fell somewhere . . . She screamed her lungs, "Ma'am, this way . . . please smile for me . . . one photo . . . only one picture . . . please . . . please?"

Ananya stood for a second and Nandita took quick pictures with her SLR.

"Thank you! . . . . Congratulations once again, ma'am!"

"Yes. I am honoured," Ananya was saying as she moved fast . . . "I am privileged to be walking with the biggies tonight." She walked away with a final wave.

Nandita stood there for some time. The crowd pushed her out. She looked at her watch; it was almost 7.30. It had been a long day. She scanned her camera. She had enough pictures for the next two days. She looked at Ananya's pictures. She had got what she wanted. She would go out, research, write a story for the cover, something her editor could never think of in years, 'An Inspirational Success Story of a Woman!'

'What did he say? Naked women sell? Get me the interviews of item numbers? Bastard F&*^^%!' On a woman's day when she had covered the story of a woman corporate leader, he wanted a half-naked model on the cover.

'I will show that bastard!' "Did somebody hear about woman power?" she screamed aloud. Four women in the crowd gave her a thumbs up signal. Nandita just laughed.

All that waiting had paid off! Her first outdoor assignment was a great success. She looked at Ananya's pictures again. 'That womaniser is going to fall for this one for sure!' She looked at the fiery eyes, the great figure. 'This lady rocks . . . man!' She was further pushed out of the maddening crowd. Without bothering to look back, she crossed the road and hopped on to her press vehicle and sped into the night!

#

Ananya's gait had an unmistakable spirit. She was tasting fame for the first time. She waved over her shoulder to the screaming media one last time before quickly following her escort into the ballroom. She could hear the media scream for yet another celebrity behind her. As she glided into the gold and bejewelled ballroom with antique crystal chandeliers, she saw a figure walk towards her.

In a beige and black suit, he was looking aristocracy personified. Tall and distinguished, Vicky towered over the rest in a way characteristic only to him. Ananya's pulse was racing fast, and her heart beat in her mouth as he neared.

"Madam, *cherie*, you look gorg," he said looking deep into her eyes. She blushed a beetroot red; his lips brushed against her cheek in greeting. He gently held her by the hand.

"Thanks," she said, weak in the knees, and added, "Mom went ahead of me."

"I have seen to it that she is seated comfortably at your table . . . Shall we proceed?" he asked.

'How could a man be so gentle and caring yet so masculine and overpowering?' Ananya wondered. Vicky was everything that a woman could ask for in a man.

"You look stunning, darling," he complimented her again. "The dress accentuates your beauty," he elaborated to make her feel comfortable; while his eyes scanned her figure, she blushed again out of desire.

"You look great!" she said, earnestly looking into his eyes. "All eyes are on you, Mr Vicky Arora!"

"All women are capital 'J' of you, Ms Ananya Bhatt," he joked, their repartee starting again.

They moved towards the front tables in the ballroom dedicated to the very special guests.

"This way please, ma'am. All the award winners and VVIPS have to be seated at the front tables," the escort told her. Ananya was escorted to the foremost of the tables. Each round table allocated for the award winners had their name and designation plates . Ananya's table was in the forefront. Her mom was occupying a chair at the table already. Vicky took a chair in between Ananya and her mom.

Ananya threw a glance around the place. Drinks and wine were doing their rounds with the waiters carrying them around. She located Richa, Nilesh, and Rajesh occupying seats around a table in the far-off right corner from the back.

As Ananya caught Richa's eye, she waved at her enthusiastically.

Ananya acknowledged her wave with a swing of her hand.

Nilesh gave Ananya a thumbs up signal.

She gave a broad smile to all of them. She felt pangs of nostalgia at their very sight again.

At exactly eight, the lights went dim. The stage erected in the front lit up in the centre with a focus light! A soft music started to play in the background.

"Ladies and gentlemen! Good evening!" said a husky female voice from the shadows.

The figure glided into view to the centre under the light, sensuously swinging to the music. Ananya recognised the famous Bollywood actress Sameira. She was dressed in a soft sizzling backless silver mermaid gown that entwined her almost 'not-there waist'; her boobs protruded like twin mountains, and she moved sensuously, adding drama to what she spoke!

"My dear friends, today's evening is a special one," Sameira began. "It's the august gathering of the most distinguished only the rare ones get to experience! This is the evening we were all waiting for." She moved a fraction forward, exposing her cleavage dramatically. **"A pen is**

mightier than a sword, and a commendable task is incomplete without appreciation' as it is truly said. We are here to bestow the most outstanding honours to the extraordinary people from the publishing industry.

"I, Sameira Khan, **welcome you to the Third National Journalists' Association Awards for Excellence!** Ladies and gentlemen, to begin with, put your hands together for the star of the evening, Mr Wilfred Karpov from Russia."

The audience were enthralled for the next half an hour with the percussionist playing the Ganesh *Vandana* in an Indo-Russian fashion. The Russian drums were played to an Indian tune as an upcoming Indian singer called Ms Rajashree Dube sang the original lyrics in Sanskrit! It was the rarest of the rare audio treats. The music took the audience to a crescendo towards the end and stopped.

The guests stood up for a standing ovation. Wilfred Karpov bowed to the audience humbly. He thanked the audience in English laced with a heavy Russian accent.

In that historic moment, Vicky moved a little closer to Ananya.

Sameira took the stage again. For the first set, Sameira called upon the president of Journalists' Association and the CEO on the stage to give away the awards.

The people who walked to the dais were as diversified as designers, journalists, photographers, models, make-up artists, or photojournalist, even an errand boy for that matter from a publishing house. After a while, the crowd started to cheer and hoot from the back! The place was heating up.

Ananya looked around, The ballroom of Taj, the stage, the happy elite people, the glamorous anchor—everything looked like a dream! It had a surreal feel to it! 'I am in the crème de la crème of the publishing industry!' she thought and caught Vicky's eye. He looked at her and smiled indulgently! Ananya's mom looked on, dazed, from her corner. Everything seemed to be a dream.

After the first segment of awards, a male figure glided on to the stage. It was Varun, the model-turned-actor-turned anchor for the evening! He had become a phenomenal success only after his first film release. He was the co-host for the evening. The crowd at the back went into a hooting spree as he came and stood along Sameira.

"I am Varun," he introduced himself. The crowd went berserk.

"I have been given the privilege today to start with an award from the glamour industry that I so much endorse. Ladies and gentlemen, put your hands together for Sabyen Shah, the best associate-editor of the popular glamour magazine *Maximum Bollywood*. I would like to add here that it sold the maximum copies and broke all the previous years' records."

Mr Sabyen came on to the stage. "Sir! Would you like to say a few words?" Varun asked.

"I would love to thank my colleagues, friends, and most importantly, the editor-in-chief, Ms Mony D'Cunha, for giving an opportunity and believing in me. I thank my parents. Without them I wouldn't be standing here." His speech was fast and simple.

More whistles and claps followed.

Now Sameira glided into focus; she said, "At the Oscars, the audience is exclusive, and so it is today. I take pride and pleasure once more to invite you all to the Oscars of the publishing industry."

Varun rejoined, "If I am not mistaken, Sameira, Oscar Awards are replete with entertainment?"

"Yes, of course! We are no less!" she said in mock agitation.

"I am dying to see, Sameira, the next part of our entertainment then . . . what it holds for us?"

"It's right here, right now." Sameira added, "Have patience, Varun." She stopped as a slight flutter of laughter came from the audience and continued, "We have a couple who enthralled audiences around the world with their dancing skills. They are going to present us the stories from the lore in the most modern fashion."

"Oh, is it?" Varun asked her, mocking, and added for the audience, "Do you want to know how? It is in the form of Argentine tango! This couple is going to depict Indian mythology in Western style. Please welcome the Ballroom couple of India—Randeep Pohankar with his supermodel wife Jameema."

There was a loud bang, and the ballroom went into total darkness except for the stage. Down came on a pulley a couple entwined, like snakes; the audience let out a cry. Jameema was in a provocative, short, sizzling, 'shoulder-less' red gown, and Randeep was in a Latin lounge suit with a shimmering silver shirt! The couple enacted fifteen different show-dances 'from their repertoire' with unique costumes depicting stories from Indian mythology. Every dance was a little show with a specific theme. They gyrated on the floor in a passionate and sensual communion, interpreting music, moving together, expressing feelings along the rhythm like a syncopated march, and at other times, listening to each other with their bodies in close proximity, giving in, withdrawing, asking, rendering, ready, balancing, but anticipating. At times, it seemed as if they were meditating together with the music. While the love stories unfolded in the dancing forms, the audience sat speechless.

The act was over after a good one and a half hours. The applause was stupendous; the lights shone on Randeep and Jameema.

Ananya had never seen anything like this before!

"Gentlemen and ladies! Please give it to the Ballroom couple Randeep and his supermodel wife Jameema! This dance was a part of the couple's tour to the US this season, and it goes without saying that it was a stupendous success."

Then more awards from different fields followed.

"Now we go to the next segment of the awards, the best subeditor."

With the mention of 'subeditor', Ananya sat up; she was still doubtful. She had to mentally pinch herself several times to affirm that she was sitting there, in fact, to receive an award! She wrung her hands in nervousness.

"Starting again with the glamour segment for subeditor category, I welcome Ms Sulakshana Mohot from *Glamour Flik* to come here to receive her award," announced Varun.

There was a huge applause, but the lady did not turn up.

Her brother collected the award for her.

He was not a good speaker, so he excused himself from giving thanks.

Half a dozen awards later, it was the turn of the best editors selected on the basis of popularity. They went fast. Ananya's heart beat faster with each award being given away. Vainly, she strained to remember her memorised speech.

Next, the show continued with a famous performance of medley by the Bollywood artists dancing to popular numbers from Hindi films in a group followed by the summoning of the chief guest for the day, a local politician, Mr Viraj Desai—a popular figure, a literati himself, and a soft-hearted, pleasant-looking gentleman in his mid-fifties, known for his social work, sense of humour, and an easy, inspiring speaking style.

He said, "When I was young, I was good at writing, but I did not take it up as a profession, but today, looking at the kind of respect a journalist is getting, I am most repentant!"

The audience laughed.

"A journalist is a boon to the society," he continued. "He is the only person who works in the constant insecurity, violence, or any unfortunate conditions like war." The audience agreed.

"In many parts of the world," he said, "press freedom exists in the twilight conditions, so I will . . . I will," he repeated in his characteristic style, "look into securing the position of a journalist in our society from this day on." The crowd hooted encouragingly. He continued, "It is the utmost duty of the people in the field to inspire the youngsters with their writings like it happened during our freedom struggle," he concluded.

Ananya whispered across to Vicky, "The spirit of patriotism is marvellous, is not it?"

Her mom clapped enthusiastically in agreement.

Vicky and Ananya exchanged glances, smiling at the elderly lady's enthusiasm.

Sameira requested the chief guest to remain on the stage to give away the next segment of awards for editors and chief editors.

The categories started with the magazines on films, modelling, lifestyle, television, advertising, in that order. Needless to say, Varun and Sameira made a great compèring pair. They asked Mr Viraj Desai to take his place in the audience after the segment was over.

Sameira and Varun were announcing in turns. "May we now request Mr Valmiki Parulekar, last year's best editor and National Award winner to come up on stage? We also request the president of the National Journalists'

Association Mr Sanjay Nag to grace the dais along with CEO and founder, Mr Saurabh Venkat."

Sameira said, "We come to the most important segment this evening now."

Varun added, "Ladies, gentlemen, and my dear friends, hold your breath, as we move to the most prestigious and outstanding award for the evening."

Ananya's pulse started racing. She feverishly opened her pouch for the paper on which she had scribbled her speech. She could not find it! She prayed fervently that her name may not be announced. Vicky took her cold palm in his and patted it gently.

Sameira and Varun, along with the other three gentlemen, moved to the centre of the stage with the mike; there was a small podium at the right side of the dais that was now visible as the lights came on.

"Ladies and gentlemen, our panel categorically worked months in advance following up on several popular magazines and their editors, looking for qualities of commitment, hunger for renovation, a vision to excel at all levels, like the authenticity of stories, catching of the eyeballs, marketing, distribution, team management, and the novelty of each issue."

At this point, Ananya looked at her team in the far-off corner and smiled.

Rajesh and Nilesh put their thumbs up. Richa was listening intently, focused.

Varun took over. "While taking into consideration the above factors and an individual's contribution to a publication, the National Association of Journalists located one magazine that spiralled through others into limelight this past year! It is one of the most sought-after lifestyle magazines, my dear friends, today."

Upon chancing it, Sameira took the mike from Varun and continued, "The association marvelled at the growth rate and popularity quotient that speaks for the leader's unmistakable dedication towards it! Besides, it is the world's most sought-after lifestyle publication that is available even in the international airports across the continents, making India proud."

Ananya's heart now slipped from its place. Vicky's grip tightened.

Varun added, "Its popularity speaks for this person's brilliance, taking it to the international level in a short span of one year. That spells out the vision it was worked on! The special jury, consisting of eminent personalities from various fields, interacted at a personal level with each shortlisted candidate before coming to a decision to give away this most outstanding honour! They found that she not only had a clear vision but had the courage to follow it. True enough, each issue touched the readers to the core, constantly igniting the curiosity and fervour for more! Needless to say, the magazine zoomed into limelight from the clobbers of anonymity!" Vicky gently squeezed Ananya's hand.

Sameira added, "This publication stands out as a platform to address and reflect our society's lifestyle issues like no other. It surpassed all barriers of assumption in growth and popularity or excellence!"

Ananya stopped breathing.

The president of the Journalists' Association took the mike on an impulse from Sameira and announced: "No other person endorsed the brand so perfectly— unparalleled and unchallenged—as she did while working on bringing a change in the product, without tampering with the expectations of the readers! Ladies and gentlemen, it's my great honour to call upon Ms Ananya Bhatt, the editor-in-chief of *AFTER TEA*, an international outstanding lifestyle magazine today . . ." His voice rose to a crescendo as he continued, "To come up here and take away the **Best Editor's National Award** for this year!"

Ananya stood up slowly. There was a huge uproar; the award was brought on a platter by a glamorous volunteer. For some reason she could not move.

"Ms Bhatt?" Varun announced again. The bulbs flashed a million times on her face with the focus lights . Ananya walked towards the stage.

"Congratulations!" said Mr Valmiki.

"We are honoured to give this, ma'am," said the president of the Journalists' Association along with the CEO of the organisation.

The crowd stood up in respect. Ananya could not see the people because of the lights but could feel hundreds of eyes boring into her. The award was a huge pen chiselled out on a metal paper. It felt cold. She could hear her name called out from a corner and some of the people in the crowd caught it and started screaming too. She stood there transfixed, unable to move.

"Ms Ananya Bhatt, please say a few words," the president was saying.

She walked slowly to the podium. She wanted to retrace her steps actually and run.

'No cuts, no editing,' she told herself. 'Now you are facing the best from the publishing industry, no going back now! You did it to yourself. Now you have only yourself!' She cursed herself as she trudged painfully towards the mike!

For a fraction of a second she looked around . . . Sameira and Varun were giving her broad artificial smiles while others looked expectantly at her with respect!

'How can they be so cool in front of a crowd?' she thought, infuriated at her own nervousness. 'Why are there speeches after awards?' she cursed mentally.

As she placed the award on the podium, her hands were cold and shivering.

She stood in front of the huge audience, transfixed. Unable to produce a single word on her own, she tried remembering some of the lines from the speech she had written. Nothing came to her. Another time she had gone blank in front of a huge crowd was in the fourth standard elocution competition. She had become a laughing stock of the entire school later. After that she had sworn herself out of speeches. In that hopeless moment, a famous line from an American soap came to her from nowhere, **'Whatever you want to say is already there in your heart!'**

It was now almost five minutes that she was standing there without a word. The audience looked at her expectantly, and she could see that some were getting restless.

"I am . . . umm umm," she mumbled.

"I . . . I was confused, alone, and penniless a year back, at the bottom of a dark well! My confidence was at its lowest, my life in shambles."

A few people let out sighs, and others looked at her quizzically with narrowed eyes.

"As my life changed overnight, I found myself at the threshold, fighting to resurrect it again, for myself and my little one. Coming back home was the only option available for me . . . I did . . . umm umm."

"What is she saying?" somebody said. "Shh!" said another. "Listen!"

Ananya continued, "Umm, I had just shut the American chapter by selling off my home abroad, embarking on a journey back home."

The audience now had a look of 'let us listen . . . to her . . . let's listen.' A hush fell over the hall.

"I did not want to take up teaching for my own reasons. I had only one option left. That was writing."

"Ohhh!" said some from the audience . . . "One person believed in me and gave me this job with *AFTER TEA*. I don't know why? I could not let him and myself down."

At that point, Ananya looked at Vicky. "Thank you!"

She continued in the same breath, "Life changed . . . overnight." It was not a typical award winner's speech, but the audience found it interesting . . . now. They sat speechless!

"The qualities which brought me here tonight were gained in the days of my working with *AFTER TEA*," Ananya continued. 'It's all there, it's all there,' she told herself nervously. 'Continue, girl,' she thought.

"The only experience I had at the time of joining was the experience of motherhood." She paused. "And a degree in English Literature."

"Ohh," the crowd sighed; a few women had soft expressions on their faces now.

"The magazine was my baby, the team my family. They looked up to me for everything. I perfected the skill to lead by example.

"Mastering the capacity to grow under difficult and contradictory circumstances . . . is the skill of a good mother. For children, mom knows everything. For my team, I knew everything! I followed this principle with confidence, and nobody questioned me in return."

Surprised laughter.

"In times of difficulty, the team looks for motivation from you to excel. Who can be a better counsellor than a parent? I became an expert counsellor for them."

"I learnt from my short experience," Ananya continued from her heart. "Trying to be as selfless as possible. With my hands-on attitude, I did not let my team rest in peace, to sit back and laze. This attitude made us work *together* towards our goals."

Vicky remembered the 'hands-on' Ananya on a rubble and wanted to laugh.

There were cheers from Richa and others.

"I truthfully felt that my team was my family and worked towards keeping them together. My days at home included a lot of pre-planning. I did the same with the publication. I planned everything beforehand. Initially, I would work on an abstract idea for an issue at hand that slowly worked itself towards my vision . . . it does not seem as easy as it sounds, but **I** . . . sorry . . . **We** accomplished," Ananya corrected herself.

By now, the cameras went full swing, capturing every word of what she was saying. "I had my moments of turmoil, confusion, and doubt. As my professional experience was nil, I depended on what truly came from the heart, and it simply worked."

The audience broke into claps.

"Believe me, not a moment did I ponder about what I would gain but went on with passion. This award is the outcome of a journey equivalent to 100 years in one . . ." She paused dramatically, and said, "**OF FINDING MYSELF!**"

Ananya fell silent for a short spell as her throat constricted . . . some people in the audience started to sob.

"Blessed he is who has found his vocation in life . . . I have found mine," Ananya whispered into the mike . . . the audience stood up.

"I have not, people," she continued, "completed my speech. I had written my speech on a piece of paper yesterday and lost it today. I must have misplaced it because I was extremely nervous . . .".

The audience laughed.

"I thank the piece of paper for getting lost . . . Mr Vicky Arora for believing in me . . . my mom, who travelled all the way from London to be here." Ananya's mom looked at her, wiping tears. The audience craned their necks to look at the people mentioned.

"My small but cute family, my whole team of *AFTER TEA*, my baby, and a wonderful person called Marriamma who takes care of her in my absence." Ananya paused.

"I love you all, thank you!" She stood there, holding the podium for support, as she found herself crying. The standing ovation went on for a long time. It was not for the speech but for a woman who was herself! The cameras started clicking, the admirers from the crowd came up on stage slowly to congratulate her personally, as Vicky and her mom looked on.

Epilogue

Six Months Later

Ananya became one of the busiest celebrities since the awards function. She is now a nominated jury member of the All India Journalists' Association. She is actively participating in the process of selecting the best editor for the coming year.

Vicky's dream project is well on its way. A 110-storey hotel has got legal permission, and he has roped in the best architects and builders from world over for constructing it.

Ananya and Vicky have come up with a wedding date.

Alia is growing up fast and attending a pre-school playgroup. Now she is almost two years old and a bundle of mischief . . . She is more attached to Vicky than anyone else.

Ananya's mom returned to UK and visits her whenever time permits.

Marriamma is still a part of the family . . . She visits her children in Kerala for short spells, and she has big plans for their education. She also has plans to live with her extended family, Ananya and Alia, as long as possible.

Acknowledgements

When a book is written, there are a 100 hands that help in so many different ways till it is complete—some are seen and some unseen. To name a few in a limited space is impossible . . .

The seen hands—Mr Durga Prasad for the support and for being . . . the love of my life . . .

Ridhima, I am grateful to her for being there, understanding, encouraging, and most important, giving an honest feedback after painstakingly reading the story word by word . . .

All my friends and extended family members . . .

The unseen hands in the order of importance . . . Shweta . . . Hemesh.

Last but not the least, my parents . . . My father specially, who is no more . . . He would have been most proud to see my book published.

A Note on the Author

Anuradha Prasad has a doctorate in English Literature from Mumbai University. She is an artist, a feature writer, and a journalist. She writes on invitation regularly. She loves blogging, counselling, observing nature, travelling, music, movies, Bollywood, and spending time with her family and friends. She lives in Mumbai with her Family.

To know more about her, please log on to www. anuradha-prasad.com

GLOSSARY

Beta—son or my child

Ganesh Vandana—a prayer to the Indian elephant God

Bhaiya—older brother

Haan—yes

Anarkali—long frock skirt top of an Indian traditional outfit

Chudidars—Indian tights worn over traditional Indian top

Ghungroo—very small anklet bells

Kamarbandhs—waist band

Kurtis—a small traditional Indian tunic

Ramayan—an Indian epic

Mahadev—name of an Indian God

Pudina—a kind of herb

Paratha—Indian stuffed bread eaten with pickle or curds.

Pulav—Indian vegetable fried rice

Raita—a curd dish

Vipassana—A type of spiritual technique for spiritual development

Maharaj—king, a guru or a learned saint

Nai, nai—no

Peepal—type of a tree

Ganesha—Indian Elephant God

Sarpanch—village head

Aai—mother in Marathi language

Bhago. Kya—run away

Kya hai—what do you want

Mafi—forgive

Bolna tha—wanted to tell

Batana hai—wanted to inform

Iske bare mein—about him

Chodo—leave

Saach Ka Samna—facing the truth

Himmatwala—name of a popular hindi movie

Naino main—in your eyes

Kajra—Indian kohl

Mein—in or into

Sajna—lover

Tanduri—Indian coal stove used for making bread

Murgi—chicken

Hoon—I am

Dabang—name of a famous hindi movie

Haan bol—say yes

Ek picture mein—In a movie

Dekha tha—saw it

Aisa hi scene—a similar scene

Kammez—type of Indian top

Dupatta—Long Indian scarf